WITCH WEEK

WITCH WEEK

Diana Wynne Jones

MACMILLAN CHILDREN'S BOOKS
London

First published 1982
Reprinted 1983 by
MACMILLAN CHILDREN'S BOOKS
A division of Macmillan Publishers Limited
London and Basingstoke

Associated companies throughout the world

Photoset by Redwood Burn Ltd
Printed by The Anchor Press Ltd,
Tiptree, Essex
Bound by Wm Brendon & Son Ltd, Tiptree, Essex

British Library Cataloguing in Publication Data

Jones, Diana Wynne
    Witch week.
    I. Title ·
    823 '.914[J]   PZ7

ISBN 0–333–33189–3

Chapter One

The note said: *SOMEONE IN THIS CLASS IS A WITCH*. It was written in capital letters in ordinary blue ballpoint, and it had appeared between two of the Geography books Mr Crossley was marking. Anyone could have written it. Mr Crossley rubbed his ginger moustache unhappily. He looked out over the bowed heads of Class 2Y and wondered what to do about it.

He decided not to take the note to the Headmistress. It was possibly just a joke, and Miss Cadwallader had no sense of humour to speak of. The person to take it to was the Deputy Head, Mr Wentworth. But the difficulty there was that Mr Wentworth's son was a member of 2Y – the small boy near the back who looked younger than the rest was Brian Wentworth. No. Mr Crossley decided to ask the writer of the note to own up. He would explain just what a serious accusation it was and leave the rest to the person's conscience.

Mr Crossley cleared his throat to speak. A number of 2Y looked up hopefully, but Mr Crossley had changed his mind by then. It was Journal time, and Journal time was only to be interrupted for a serious emergency. Larwood House was very strict about that rule. Larwood House was very strict about a lot of things, because it was a boarding school run by the government for witch-orphans and children with other problems. The journals were to help the children with their problems. They were supposed to be strictly private. Every day, for half an hour, every pupil had to confide his or her private thoughts to their journal, and nothing else was done until everyone had. Mr Crossley admired the idea heartily.

But the real reason that Mr Crossley changed his mind was the awful thought that the note might be true. Someone in 2Y could easily be a witch. Only Miss Cadwallader knew who exactly in 2Y was a witch-orphan, but Mr Crossley suspected that a lot of them were. Other classes had given Mr Crossley feelings of pride and pleasure in being a schoolmaster. 2Y never did. Only two of them gave him any pride at all: Theresa Mullett and Simon Silverson. They were both model pupils. The rest of the girls tailed dismally off until you came to empty chatterers like Estelle Green, or that dumpy girl, Nan Pilgrim, who was definitely the odd one out. The boys were divided into groups. Some had the sense to follow Simon Silverson's example, but quite as many clustered round that bad boy Dan Smith, and others again admired that tall Indian boy, Nirupam Singh. Or they were loners like Brian Wentworth and that unpleasant boy Charles Morgan.

Here Mr Crossley looked at Charles Morgan and Charles Morgan looked back, with one of the blank, nasty looks he was famous for. Charles wore glasses, which enlarged the nasty look and trained it on Mr Crossley like a double laser beam. Mr Crossley looked away hastily and went back to worrying about the note. Everyone in 2Y gave up hoping for anything interesting to happen and went back to their journals.

28 October 1981, Theresa Mullett wrote in round, angelic writing. *Mr Crossley has found a note in our Geography books. I thought it might be from Miss Hodge at first, because we all know Teddy is dying for love of her, but he looks so worried that I think it must be from some silly girl like Estelle Green. Nan Pilgrim couldn't get over the vaulting-horse again today. She jumped and stuck halfway. It made us all laugh.*

Simon Silverson wrote: *28. 10. 81. I would like to know who put that note in the Geography books. It fell out when I was collecting them and I put it back in. If it was found lying about we could all be blamed. This is strictly off the record of course.*

I do not know, Nirupam Singh wrote musingly, *how anyone manages to write much in their journal, since everyone knows Miss Cadwallader reads them all during the holidays. I do not write my secret thoughts. I will now describe the Indian rope trick which I saw in India before my father came to live in England...*

Two desks away from Nirupam, Dan Smith chewed his pen a great deal and finally wrote, *Well I mean it's not much good if you've got to write your secret feelings, what I mean is it takes all the joy out of it and you don't know what to write. It means they aren't secret if you see what I mean.*

I do not think, Estelle Green wrote, *that I have any secret feelings today, but I would like to know what is in the note from Miss Hodge that Teddy has just found. I thought she scorned him utterly.*

At the back of the room, Brian Wentworth wrote, sighing, *Timetables just run away with me, that is my problem. During Geography I planned a bus journey from London to Baghdad via Paris. Next lesson I shall plan the same journey via Berlin.*

Nan Pilgrim meanwhile was scrawling, *This is a message to the person who reads our journals. Are you Miss Cadwallader, or does Miss Cadwallader make Mr Wentworth do it?* She stared at what she had written, rather taken aback at her own daring. This kind of thing happened to her sometimes. Still, she thought, there were hundreds of journals and hundreds of daily entries. The chances of Miss Cadwallader reading this one had to be very small — particularly if she went on and made it really boring. *I shall now be boring,* she wrote. *Teddy Crossley's real name is Harold, but he got called Teddy*

3

out of the hymn that goes 'Gladly my cross I'd bear.' But of course everyone sings 'Crossley my glad-eyed bear.' Mr Crossley is glad-eyed. He thinks everyone should be upright and honourable and interested in Geography. I am sorry for him.

But the one who was best at making his journal boring was Charles Morgan. His entry read, *I got up. I felt hot at breakfast. I do not like porridge. Second lesson was Woodwork but not for long. I think we have Games next.*

Looking at this, you might think Charles was either very stupid or very muddled, or both. Anyone in 2Y would have told you that it had been a chilly morning and there had been cornflakes for breakfast. Second lesson had been PE, during which Nan Pilgrim had so much amused Theresa Mullett by failing to jump the horse, and the lesson to come was Music, not Games. But Charles was not writing about the day's work. He really was writing about his secret feelings, but he was doing it in his own private code so that no one could know.

He started every entry with *I got up.* It meant, I hate this school. When he wrote *I do not like porridge*, that was actually true, but porridge was his code-word for Simon Silverson. Simon was porridge at breakfast, potatoes at lunch, and bread at tea. All the other people he hated had code-words too. Dan Smith was cornflakes, cabbage and butter. Theresa Mullett was milk.

But when Charles wrote *I felt hot*, he was not talking about school at all. He meant he was remembering the witch being burnt. It was a thing that would keep coming into his head whenever he was not thinking of anything else, much as he tried to forget it. He had been so young that he had been in a pushchair. His big sister Bernadine had been pushing him while his mother carried the shopping, and they had been crossing a road where there was a view down into the Market Square.

4

There were crowds of people down there, and a sort of flickering. Bernadine had stopped the pushchair in the middle of the street in order to stare. She and Charles had just time to glimpse the bone-fire starting to burn, and they had seen that the witch was a large fat man. Then their mother came rushing back and scolded Bernadine on across the road. "You mustn't look at witches!" she said. "Only awful people do that!" So Charles had only seen the witch for an instant. He never spoke about it, but he never forgot it. It always astonished him that Bernadine seemed to forget about it completely. What Charles was really saying in his journal was that the witch came into his head during breakfast, until Simon Silverson made him forget again by eating all the toast.

When he wrote *Woodwork second lesson*, he meant that he had gone on to think about the second witch – which was a thing he did not think about so often. *Woodwork* was anything Charles liked. They only had Woodwork once a week, and Charles had chosen that for his code on the very reasonable grounds that he was not likely to enjoy anything at Larwood House any oftener than that. Charles had liked the second witch. She had been quite young and rather pretty, in spite of her torn skirt and untidy hair. She had come scrambling across the wall at the end of the garden and stumbled down the rockery to the lawn, carrying her smart shoes in one hand. Charles had been nine years old then, and he was minding his little brother on the lawn. Luckily for the witch, his parents were out.

Charles knew she was a witch. She was out of breath and obviously frightened. He could hear the yells and police whistles in the houses behind. Besides, who else but a witch would run away from the police in the middle of the afternoon in a tight skirt? But he made quite sure. He said, "Why are you running away in our garden?"

The witch rather desperately hopped on one foot. She

5

had a large blister on the other foot, and both her stockings were laddered. "I'm a witch," she panted. "Please help me, little boy!"

"Why can't you magic yourself safe?" Charles asked.

"Because I can't when I'm this frightened!" gasped the witch. "I tried, but it just went wrong! *Please*, little boy – sneak me out through your house and don't say a word, and I'll give you luck for the rest of your life. I promise."

Charles looked at her in that intent way of his which most people found blank and nasty. He saw she was speaking the truth. He saw, too, that she understood the look as very few people seemed to. "Come in through the kitchen," he said. And he led the witch, hobbling on her blister in her laddered stockings, through the kitchen and down the hall to the front door.

"Thanks," she said. "You're a love." She smiled at him while she put her hair right in the hall mirror, and, after she had done something to her skirt that may have been witchcraft to make it seem untorn again, she bent down and kissed Charles. "If I get away, I'll bring you luck," she said. Then she put her smart shoes on again and went away down the front garden, trying hard not to limp. At the front gate, she waved and smiled at Charles.

That was the end of the part Charles liked. That was why he wrote *But not for long* next. He never saw the witch again, or heard what had happened to her. He ordered his little brother never to say a word about her – and Graham obeyed, because he always did everything Charles said – and then he watched and waited for any sign of the witch or any sign of luck. None came. It was next to impossible for Charles to find out what might have happened to the witch, because there had been new laws since he glimpsed the first witch burning. There were no more public burnings. The bone-fires were lit inside the walls of gaols instead, and the radio would simply announce: "Two witches were burnt this

6

morning inside Holloway Gaol." Every time Charles heard this kind of announcement he thought it was *his* witch. It gave him a blunt, hurtful feeling inside. He thought of the way she had kissed him, and he was fairly sure it made you wicked too, to be kissed by a witch. He gave up expecting to be lucky. In fact, to judge from the amount of bad luck he had had, he thought the witch must have been caught almost straight away. For the blunt, hurtful feeling he had when the radio announced a burning made him refuse to do anything his parents told him to do. He just gave them his steady stare instead. And each time he stared, he knew they thought he was being nasty. They did not understand it the way the witch did. And, since Graham imitated everything Charles did, Charles's parents very soon decided Charles was a problem child and leading Graham astray. They arranged for him to be sent to Larwood House, because it was quite near.

When Charles wrote *Games*, he meant bad luck. Like everyone else in 2Y, he had seen Mr Crossley had found a note. He did not know what was in the note, but when he looked up and caught Mr Crossley's eye, he knew it meant bad luck coming.

Mr Crossley still could not decide what to do about the note. If what it said was true, that meant Inquisitors coming to the school. And that was a thoroughly frightening thought. Mr Crossley sighed and put the note in his pocket. "Right, everyone," he said. "Put away your journals and get into line for Music."

As soon as 2Y had shuffled away to the school hall, Mr Crossley sped to the staff room, hoping to find someone he could consult about the note.

He was lucky enough to find Miss Hodge there. As Theresa Mullett and Estelle Green had observed, Mr Crossley was in love with Miss Hodge. But of course he never let it show. Probably the only person in the school who did not seem to know was Miss Hodge herself. Miss

Hodge was a small neat person who wore neat grey skirts and blouses, and her hair was even neater and smoother than Theresa Mullett's. She was busy making neat stacks of books on the staff room table, and she went on making them all the time Mr Crossley was telling her excitedly about the note. She spared the note one glance.

"No, I can't tell who wrote it either," she said.

"But what shall I do about it?" Mr Crossley pleaded. "Even if it's true, it's such a spiteful thing to write! And suppose it *is* true. Suppose one of them is—" He was in a pitiable state. He wanted so badly to attract Miss Hodge's attention, but he knew that words like *witch* were not the kind of words one used in front of a lady. "I don't like to say it in front of you."

"I was brought up to be sorry for witches," Miss Hodge remarked calmly.

"Oh, so was I! We all are," Mr Crossley said hastily. "I just wondered how I should handle it—"

Miss Hodge lined up another stack of books. "I think it's just a silly joke," she said. "Ignore it. Aren't you supposed to be teaching 4X?"

"Yes, yes. I suppose I am," Mr Crossley agreed miserably. And he was forced to hurry away without Miss Hodge having looked at him once.

Miss Hodge thoughtfully squared off another stack of books, until she was sure Mr Crossley had gone. Then she smoothed her smooth hair and hurried away upstairs to find Mr Wentworth.

Mr Wentworth, as Deputy Head, had a study where he wrestled with the timetable and various other problems Miss Cadwallader gave him. When Miss Hodge tapped on the door, he was wrestling with a particularly fierce one. There were seventy people in the school orchestra. Fifty of these were also in the school choir and twenty of those fifty were in the school play. Thirty boys in the orchestra were in various football teams, and twenty of the girls played hockey for the school. At least a third played basketball as well. The volleyball team were all in the school play. Problem: how do you arrange rehearsals and practices without asking most people to be in three places at once? Mr Wentworth rubbed the thin patch at the back of his hair despairingly. "Come in," he said. He saw the bright, smiling, anxious face of Miss Hodge, but his mind was not on her at all.

"So spiteful of someone, and so awful if it's true!" he heard Miss Hodge saying. And then, merrily, "But I think I have a scheme to discover who wrote the note – it must be someone in 2Y. Can we put our heads together and work it out, Mr Wentworth?" She put her own head on one side, invitingly.

Mr Wentworth had no idea what she was talking about. He scratched the place where his hair was going and stared at her. Whatever it was, it had all the marks of a scheme that ought to be squashed. "People only write anonymous notes to make themselves feel important," he said experimentally. "You mustn't take them seriously."

"But it's the perfect scheme!" Miss Hodge protested. "If I can explain—"

Not squashed yet, whatever it is, thought Mr Wentworth. "No. Just tell me the exact words of this note," he said.

Miss Hodge instantly became crushed and shocked. "But it's awful!" Her voice fell to a dramatic whisper. "It says someone in 2Y is a witch!"

Mr Wentworth realized that his instinct had been right. "What did I tell you?" he said heartily. "That's the sort of stuff you can only ignore, Miss Hodge."

"But someone in 2Y has a very sick mind!" Miss Hodge whispered.

Mr Wentworth considered 2Y, including his own son Brian. "They all have," he said. "Either they'll grow out of it, or we'll see them all riding round on broomsticks in the sixth form." Miss Hodge started back. She was genuinely shocked at this coarse language. But she hastily made herself laugh. She could see it was a joke. "Take no notice," said Mr Wentworth. "Ignore it, Miss Hodge." And he went back to his problem with some relief.

Miss Hodge went back to her stacks of books, not as crushed as Mr Wentworth supposed she was. Mr Wentworth had made a joke to her. He had never done that before. She must be getting somewhere. For – and this was a fact not known to Theresa Mullett or Estelle Green – Miss Hodge intended to marry Mr Wentworth. He was a widower. When Miss Cadwallader retired, Miss Hodge was sure Mr Wentworth would be Head of Larwood House. This suited Miss Hodge, who had her old father to consider. For this, she was quite willing to put up with Mr Wentworth's bald patch and his tense and harrowed look. The only drawback was that putting up with Mr Wentworth also meant putting up with Brian. A little frown wrinkled Miss Hodge's smooth forehead at the thought of Brian Wentworth. Now there was a boy who quite deserved the way the rest of 2Y were always on to him. Never mind. He could be sent away to another school.

Meanwhile, in Music, Mr Brubeck was asking Brian to sing on his own. 2Y had trailed their way through 'Here we sit like birds in the wilderness'. They had made it sound like a lament. "I'd prefer a wilderness to this place," Estelle Green whispered to her friend Karen Grigg. Then they sang 'Cuckaburra sits in the old gum tree'. That sounded like a funeral dirge. "What's a cuckaburra?" Karen whispered to Estelle.

"Another kind of bird," Estelle whispered back. "Australian."

"No, no *no*!" shouted Mr Brubeck. "Brian is the only one of you who doesn't sound like a cockerel with a sore throat!"

10

"Mr Brubeck must have birds on the brain!" Estelle giggled. And Simon Silverson, who believed, strongly and sincerely, that nobody was worthy of praise except himself, gave Brian a scathingly jeering look.

But Mr Brubeck was far too addicted to music to take any notice of what the rest of 2Y thought. "'The Cuckoo is a pretty bird'," he announced. "I want Brian to sing this to you on his own."

Estelle giggled, because it was birds again. Theresa giggled too, because anyone who stood out for any reason struck her as exceedingly funny. Brian stood up with the song book in his hands. He was never embarrassed. But instead of singing, he read the words out in an incredulous voice.

"'The cuckoo is a pretty bird, she singeth as she flies. She bringeth us good tidings, she telleth us no lies.' Sir, why are all these songs about birds?" he asked innocently. Charles thought that was a shrewd move of Brian's, after the way Simon Silverson had looked at him.

But it did Brian no good. He was too unpopular. Most of the girls said, "*Brian*!" in shocked voices. Simon said it jeeringly.

"Quiet!" shouted Mr Brubeck. "Brian, get on and sing!" He struck notes on the piano.

Brian stood with the book in his hands, obviously wondering what to do. It was clear that he would be in trouble with Mr Brubeck if he did not sing, and that he would be hit afterwards if he did. And while Brian hesitated, the witch in 2Y took a hand. One of the long windows of the hall flew open with a clap and let in a stream of birds. Most of them were ordinary birds: sparrows, starlings, pigeons, blackbirds and thrushes, swooping round the hall in vast numbers and shedding feathers and droppings as they swooped. But among the beating wings were two curious furry creatures with large pouches, which kept uttering violent laughing

11

sounds, and the red and yellow thing swooping among a cloud of sparrows and shouting "Cuckoo!" was clearly a parrot.

Luckily, Mr Brubeck thought it was simply the wind which had let the birds in. The rest of the lesson had to be spent in chasing the birds out again. By that time, the laughing birds with pouches had vanished. Evidently the witch had decided they were a mistake. But everyone in 2Y had clearly seen them. Simon said importantly, "If this happens again, we all ought to get together and—"

At this, Nirupam Singh turned round, towering among the beating wings. "Have you any proof that this is not perfectly natural?" he said.

Simon had not, so he said no more.

By the end of the lesson, all the birds had been sent out of the window again, except the parrot. The parrot escaped to a high curtain rail, where no one could reach it, and sat there shouting "Cuckoo!" Mr Brubeck sent 2Y away and called the caretaker to get rid of it. Charles trudged away with the rest, thinking that this must be the end of the Games he had predicted in his journal. But he was quite wrong. It was only the beginning.

And when the caretaker came grumbling along with his small white dog trailing at his heels, to get rid of the parrot, the parrot had vanished.

Chapter Two

The next day was the day Miss Hodge tried to find out who had written the note. It was also the worst day either Nan Pilgrim or Charles Morgan had ever spent at Larwood House. It did not begin too badly for Charles, but Nan was late for breakfast.

She had broken her shoelace. She was told off by Mr Towers for being late, and then by a prefect. By this time, the only table with a place was one where all the others were boys. Nan slid into the place, horribly embarrassed. They had eaten all the toast already, except one slice. Simon Silverson took that slice as Nan arrived. "Bad luck, fatso." From further down the table, Nan saw Charles Morgan looking at her. It was meant to be a look of sympathy, but, like all Charles's looks, it came out like a blank double-barrelled glare. Nan pretended not to see it and did her best to eat wet, pale scrambled egg on its own.

At lessons, she discovered that Theresa and her friends had started a new craze. That was a bad sign. They were always more than usually pleased with themselves at the start of a craze — even though this one had probably started so that they need not think of witches or birds. The craze was white knitting, white and clean and fluffy, which you kept wrapped in a towel so that it would stay clean. The classroom filled with mutters of, "Two purl, one plain, twist two..."

But the day really got into its evil stride in the middle of the morning, during PE. Larwood House had that every day, like the journals. 2Y joined with 2X and 2Z, and the boys went running in the field, while the girls went together to the Gym. The climbing-ropes were let down there.

Theresa and Estelle and the rest gave glad cries and went shinning up the ropes with easy swinging pulls. Nan tried to lurk out of sight against the wall-bars. Her heart fell with a flop into her gym-shoes. This was worse even than the vaulting-horse. Nan simply could not climb ropes. She had been born without the proper muscles or something.

And, since it was that kind of day, Miss Phillips spotted Nan almost at once. "Nan, you haven't had a turn yet. Theresa, Delia, Estelle, come on down and let Nan have her turn on the ropes." Theresa and the rest came down readily. They knew they were about to see some fun.

Nan saw their faces and ground her teeth. This time, she vowed, she would do it. She would climb right up to the ceiling and wipe that grin off Theresa's face. Nevertheless, the distance to the ropes seemed several hundred shiny yards. Nan's legs, in the floppy divided skirts they wore for Gym, had gone mauve and wide, and her arms felt like weak pink puddings. When she reached the rope, the knot on the end of it seemed to hang rather higher than her head. And she was supposed to stand on that knot somehow.

She gripped the rope in her fat, weak hands and jumped. All that happened was that the knot hit her heavily in the chest and her feet dropped sharply to the floor again. A murmur of amusement began among Theresa and her friends. Nan could hardly believe it. This was ridiculous – worse than usual! She could not even get off the floor now. She took a new grip on the rope and jumped again. And again. And again. And she leapt and leapt, bounding like a floppy kangaroo, and still the knot kept hitting her in the chest and her feet

14

kept hitting the floor. The murmurs of the rest grew into giggles and then to outright laughter. Until at last, when Nan was almost ready to give up, her feet somehow found the knot, groped, gripped and hung on. And there she clung, upside down like a sloth, breathless and sweating, from arms which did not seem to work any more. This was terrible. And she still had to climb up the rope. She wondered whether to fall off on her back and die.

Miss Phillips was beside her. "Come on, Nan. Stand up on the knot."

Somehow, feeling it was superhuman of her, Nan managed to lever herself upright. She stood there, wobbling gently round in little circles, while Miss Phillips, with her face level with Nan's trembling knees, kindly and patiently explained for the hundredth time exactly how to climb a rope.

Nan clenched her teeth. She *would* do it. Everyone else did. It must be possible. She shut her eyes to shut out the other girls' grinning faces and did as Miss Phillips told her. She took a strong and careful grip on the rope above her head. Carefully, she put rope between the top of one foot and the bottom of the other. She kept her eyes shut. Firmly, she pulled with her arms. Crisply, she pulled her feet up behind. Gripped again. Reached up again, with fearful concentration. Yes, this was it! She was doing it at last! The secret must be to keep your eyes shut. She gripped and pulled. She could feel her body easily swinging upwards towards the ceiling, just as the others did it.

But, around her, the giggles grew to laughter, and the laughter grew into screams, then shouts, and became a perfect storm of hilarity. Puzzled, Nan opened her eyes. All round her, at knee-level, she saw laughing red faces, tears running out of eyes, and people doubled over yelling with mirth. Even Miss Phillips was biting her lip and snorting a little. And small wonder. Nan looked

15

down to find her gym-shoes still resting on the knot at the bottom of the rope. After all that climbing, she was still standing on the knot.

Nan tried to laugh too. She was sure it had been very funny. But it was hard to be amused. Her only consolation was that, after that, none of the other girls could climb the ropes either. They were too weak with laughing.

The boys, meanwhile, were running round and round the field. They were stripped to little pale-blue running shorts and splashing through the dew in big spiked shoes. It was against the rules to run in anything but spikes. They were divided into little groups of labouring legs. The quick group of legs in front, with muscles, belonged to Simon Silverson and his friends, and to Brian Wentworth. Brian was a good runner in spite of his short legs. Brian was prudently trying to keep to the rear of Simon, but every so often the sheer joy of running overcame him and he went ahead. Then he would get bumped and jostled by Simon's friends, for everyone knew it was Simon's right to be in front.

The group of legs behind these were paler and moved without enthusiasm. These belonged to Dan Smith and his friends. All of them could have run at least as fast as Simon Silverson, but they were saving themselves for better things. They loped along easily, chatting among themselves. Today, they kept bursting into laughter.

Behind these again laboured an assorted group of legs: mauve legs, fat legs, bright white legs, legs with no muscles at all, and the great brown legs of Nirupam Singh, which seemed too heavy for the rest of Nirupam's skinny body to lift. Everyone in this group was too breathless to talk. Their faces wore assorted expressions of woe.

The last pair of legs, far in the rear, belonged to Charles Morgan. There was nothing particularly wrong with Charles's legs, except that his feet were in ordinary school-shoes and soaked through. He was always behind. He chose to be. This was one of the few times in the day when he could be alone to think. He had discovered that, as long as he was thinking of something else, he could keep up his slow trot for hours. And think. The only interruptions he had to fear were when the other groups came pounding past him and he was tangled up in their efforts for a few seconds. Or when Mr Towers, encased in his nice warm tracksuit, came loping up alongside and called ill-advised encouragements to Charles.

So Charles trotted slowly on, thinking. He gave himself over to hating Larwood House. He hated the field under his feet, the shivering autumn trees that dripped on him, the white goalposts, and the neat line of pine trees in front of the spiked wall that kept everyone in. Then, when he swung round the corner and had a view of the school buildings, he hated them more. They were built of a purplish sort of brick. Charles thought it was the colour a person's face would go if they were throttling. He thought of the long corridors inside, painted caterpillar green, the thick radiators which were never warm, the brown classrooms, the frosty white dormitories, and the smell of school food, and he was almost in an ecstasy of hate. Then he looked at the groups of legs straggling round the field ahead, and he hated all the people in the school most horribly of all.

Upon that, he found he was remembering the witch being burnt. It swept into his head unbidden, as it always did. Only today, it seemed worse than usual. Charles found he was remembering things he had not noticed at the time: the exact shape of the flames, just leaping from small to large, and the way the fat man who was a witch had bent sideways away from them. He could see the man's exact face, the rather blobby nose with a wart on it, the sweat on it, and the flames shining off the man's eyes and the sweat. Above all, he could see the man's

17

expression. It was astounded. The fat man had not believed he was going to die until the moment Charles saw him. He must have thought his witchcraft could save him. Now he knew it could not. And he was horrified. Charles was horrified too. He trotted along in a sort of trance of horror.

But here was the smart red tracksuit of Mr Towers loping along beside him. "Charles, what are you doing running in walking-shoes?"

The fat witch vanished. Charles should have been glad, but he was not. His thinking had been interrupted, and he was not private any more.

"I said why aren't you wearing your spikes?" Mr Towers said.

Charles slowed down a little while he wondered what to reply. Mr Towers trotted springily beside him, waiting for an answer. Because he was not thinking any more, Charles found his legs aching and his chest sore. That annoyed him. He was even more annoyed about his spikes. He knew Dan Smith had hidden them. That was why that group were laughing. Charles could see their faces craning over their shoulders as they ran, to see what he was telling Mr Towers. That annoyed him even more. Charles did not usually have this kind of trouble, the way Brian Wentworth did. His double-barrelled nasty look had kept him safe up to now, if lonely. But he foresaw he was going to have to think of something more than just looking in future. He felt very bitter.

"I couldn't find my spikes, sir."

"How hard did you look?"

"Everywhere," Charles said bitterly. Why don't I say it was them? he wondered. And knew the answer. Life would not be worth living for the rest of term.

"In my experience," said Mr Towers, running and talking as easily as if he were sitting still, "when a lazy boy like you says everywhere, it means nowhere. Report to me in the locker room after school and find those

18

spikes. You stay there until you find them. Right?"

"Yes," said Charles. Bitterly, he watched Mr Towers surge away from him and run up beside the next group to pester Nirupam Singh.

He hunted for his spikes again during break. But it was hopeless. Dan had hidden them somewhere really cunning. At least, after break, Dan Smith had something else to laugh about beside Charles. Nan Pilgrim soon found out what. As Nan came into the classroom for lessons, she was greeted by Nirupam. "Hallo," asked Nirupam. "Will you do your rope trick for me too?"

Nan gave him a glare that was mostly astonishment and pushed past him without replying. How did he know about the ropes? she thought. The girls just never talked to the boys! How *did* he know?

But next moment, Simon Silverson came up to Nan, barely able to stop laughing. "My dear Dulcinea!" he said. "What a charming name you have! Were you called after the Archwitch?" After that, he doubled up with laughter, and so did most of the people near.

"Her name really is Dulcinea, you know," Nirupam said to Charles.

This was true. Nan's face felt to her like a balloon on fire. Nothing else, she was sure, could be so large and so hot. Dulcinea Wilkes had been the most famous witch of all time. No one was supposed to know Nan's name was Dulcinea. She could not think how it had leaked out. She tried to stalk loftily away to her desk, but she was caught by person after person, all laughingly calling out, "Hey, Dulcinea!" She did not manage to sit down until Mr Wentworth was already in the room.

2Y usually attended during Mr Wentworth's lessons. He was known to be absolutely merciless. Besides, he had a knack of being interesting, which made his lessons seem shorter than other teachers'. But today, no one could keep their mind on Mr Wentworth. Nan was trying not to cry. When, a year ago, Nan's aunts had brought her to Larwood House, even softer, plumper and more timid than she was now, Miss Cadwallader had promised that no one should know her name was Dulcinea. Miss Cadwallader had *promised*! So how had someone found out? The rest of 2Y kept breaking into laughter and excited whispers. Could Nan Pilgrim be a witch? Fancy anyone being called Dulcinea! It was as bad as being called Guy Fawkes! Halfway through the lesson, Theresa Mullett was so overcome by the thought of Nan's name that she was forced to bury her face in her knitting to laugh.

Mr Wentworth promptly took the knitting away. He dumped the clean white bundle on the desk in front of him and inspected it dubiously. "What is it about this that seems so funny?" He unrolled the towel – at which Theresa gave a faint yell of dismay – and held up a very small fluffy thing with holes in it. "Just what is this?"

Everyone laughed.

"It's a bootee!" Theresa said angrily.

"Who for?" retorted Mr Wentworth.

Everyone laughed again. But the laughter was short and guilty, because everyone knew Theresa was not to be laughed at.

Mr Wentworth seemed unaware that he had performed a miracle and made everyone laugh at Theresa, instead of the other way round. He cut the laughter even shorter by telling Dan Smith to come out to the blackboard and show him two triangles that were alike. The lesson went on. Theresa kept muttering, "It's not funny! It's just not funny!" Every time she said it, her friends nodded sympathetically, while the rest of the class kept looking at Nan and bursting into muffled laughter.

At the end of the lesson, Mr Wentworth uttered a few unpleasant remarks about mass punishments if people behaved like this again. Then, as he turned to leave, he said, "And by the way, if Charles Morgan, Nan Pilgrim and Nirupam Singh haven't already looked at the main

20

notice board, they should do so at once. They will find they are down for lunch on high table."

Both Nan and Charles knew then that this was not just a bad day – it was the worst day ever. Miss Cadwallader sat at high table with any important visitors to the school. It was her custom to choose three pupils from the school every day to sit there with her. This was so that everyone should learn proper table manners, and so that Miss Cadwallader should get to know her pupils. It was rightly considered a terrible ordeal. Neither Nan nor Charles had ever been chosen before. Scarcely able to believe it, they went to check with the notice board. Sure enough it read: *Charles Morgan 2Y, Dulcinea Pilgrim 2Y, Nirupam Singh 2Y.*

Nan stared at it. So that was how everyone knew her name! Miss Cadwallader had forgotten. She had forgotten who Nan was and everything she had promised, and when she came to stick a pin in the register – or whatever she did to choose people for high table – she had simply written down the names that came under her pin.

Nirupam was looking at the notice too. He had been chosen before, but he was no less gloomy than Charles or Nan. "You have to comb your hair and get your blazer clean," he said. "And it really is true you have to eat with the same kind of knife or fork that Miss Cadwallader does. You have to watch and see what she uses all the time."

Nan stood there, letting other people looking at the notices push her about. She was terrified. She suddenly knew she was going to behave very badly on high table. She was going to drop her dinner, or scream, or maybe take all her clothes off and dance among the plates. And she was terrified, because she knew she was not going to be able to stop herself.

She was still terrified when she arrived at high table with Charles and Nirupam. They had all combed their heads sore and tried to clean from the fronts of their

21

blazers the dirt which always mysteriously arrives on the fronts of blazers, but they all felt grubby and small beside the stately company at high table. There were a number of teachers, and the Bursar, and an important-looking man called Lord Something-or-other, and tall, stringy Miss Cadwallader herself. Miss Cadwallader smiled at them graciously and pointed to three empty chairs at her left side. All of them instantly dived for the chair furthest away from Miss Cadwallader. Nan, much to her surprise, won it, and Charles won the chair in the middle, leaving Nirupam to sit beside Miss Cadwallader.

"Now we know that won't do, don't we?" said Miss Cadwallader. "We always sit with a gentleman on either side of a lady, don't we? Dulcimer must sit in the middle, and I'll have the gentleman I haven't yet met nearest me. Clive Morgan, isn't it? That's right."

Sullenly, Charles and Nan changed their places. They stood there, while Miss Cadwallader was saying grace, looking out over the heads of the rest of the school, not very far below, but far enough to make a lot of difference. Perhaps I'm going to faint, Nan thought hopefully. She still knew she was going to behave badly, but she felt very odd as well – and fainting was a fairly respectable way of behaving badly.

She was still conscious at the end of grace. She sat down with the rest, between the glowering Charles and Nirupam. Nirupam had gone pale yellow with dread. To their relief, Miss Cadwallader at once turned to the important lord and began making gracious conversation with him. The ladies from the kitchen brought round a tray of little bowls and handed everybody one.

What was this? It was certainly not a usual part of school dinner. They looked suspiciously at the bowls. They were full of yellow stuff, not quite covering little pink things.

"I believe it may be prawns," Nirupam said

22

dubiously. "For a starter."

Here Miss Cadwallader reached forth a gracious hand. Their heads at once craned round to see what implement she was going to eat out of the bowl with. Her hand picked up a fork. They picked up forks too. Nan poked hers cautiously into her bowl. Instantly she began to behave badly. She could not stop herself. "I think it's custard," she said loudly. "Do prawns mix with custard?" She put one of the pink things into her mouth. It felt rubbery. "Chewing gum?" she asked. "No, I think they're jointed worms. Worms in custard."

"Shut up!" hissed Nirupam.

"But it's not custard," Nan continued. She could hear her voice saying it, but there seemed no way to stop it. "The tongue-test proves that the yellow stuff has a strong taste of sour armpits, combined with – yes – just a touch of old drains. It comes from the bottom of a dustbin."

Charles glared at her. He felt sick. If he had dared, he would have stopped eating at once. But Miss Cadwallader continued gracefully forking up prawns – unless they really were jointed worms – and Charles did not dare do differently. He wondered how he was going to put this in his journal. He had never hated Nan Pilgrim particularly before, so he had no code-word for her. Prawn? Could he call her prawn? He choked down another worm –prawn, that was – and wished he could push the whole bowful in Nan's face.

"A clean yellow dustbin," Nan announced. "The kind they keep the dead fish for Biology in."

"Prawns are eaten curried in India," Nirupam said loudly.

Nan knew he was trying to shut her up. With a great effort, by cramming several forkfuls of worms – prawns, that was – into her mouth at once, she managed to stop herself talking. She could hardly bring herself to swallow the mouthful, but at least it kept her quiet. Most fervent-

23

ly, she hoped that the next course would be something ordinary, which she would not have any urge to describe, and so did Nirupam and Charles.

But alas! What came before them in platefuls next was one of the school kitchen's more peculiar dishes. They produced it about once a month and its official name was hot-pot. With it, came tinned peas and tinned tomatoes. Charles's head and Nirupam's craned towards Miss Cadwallader again to see what they were supposed to eat this with. Miss Cadwallader picked up a fork. They picked up forks too, and then craned a second time, to make sure that Miss Cadwallader was not going to pick up a knife as well and so make it easier for everyone. She was not. Her fork drove gracefully under a pile of tinned peas. They sighed, and found both their heads turning towards Nan then in a sort of horrified expectation.

They were not disappointed. As Nan levered loose the first greasy ring of potato, the urge to describe came upon her again. It was as if she was possessed. "Now the aim of this dish," she said, "is to use up leftovers. You take old potatoes and soak them in washing-up water that has been used at least twice. The water must be thoroughly scummy." It's like the gift of tongues! she thought. Only in my case it's the gift of foul-mouth. "Then you take a dirty old tin and rub it round with socks that have been worn for a fortnight. You fill this tin with alternate layers of scummy potatoes and cat-food, mixed with anything else you happen to have. Old doughnuts and dead flies have been used in this case—"

Could his code-word for Nan be hot-pot? Charles wondered. It suited her. No, because they only had hot-pot once a month – fortunately – and, at this rate, he would need to hate Nan practically every day. Why didn't someone stop her? Couldn't Miss Cadwallader hear?

"Now these things," Nan continued, stabbing her

24

fork into a tinned tomato, "are small creatures that have been killed and cleverly skinned. Notice, when you taste them, the slight, sweet savour of their blood—"

Nirupam uttered a small moan and went yellower than ever.

The sound made Nan look up. Hitherto, she had been staring at the table where her plate was, in a daze of terror. Now she saw Mr Wentworth sitting opposite her across the table. He could hear her perfectly. She could tell from the expression on his face. Why doesn't he stop me? she thought. Why do they let me go on? Why doesn't somebody do something, like a thunderbolt strike me, or eternal detention? Why don't I get under the table and crawl away? And, all the time, she could hear herself talking. "These did in fact start life as peas. But they have since undergone a long and deadly process. They lie for six months in a sewer, absorbing fluids and rich tastes, which is why they are called processed peas. Then—"

Here, Miss Cadwallader turned gracefully to them. Nan, to her utter relief, stopped in mid-process. "You have all been long enough in the school by now," Miss Cadwallader said, "to know the town quite well. Do you know that lovely old house in the High Street?"

They all three stared at her. Charles gulped down a ring of potato. "Lovely old house?"

"It's called the Old Gate House," said Miss Cadwallader. "It used to be part of the gate in the old town wall. A very lovely old brick building."

"You mean the one with a tower on top and windows like a church?" Charles asked, though he could not think why Miss Cadwallader should talk of this and not processed peas.

"That's the one," said Miss Cadwallader. "And it's such a shame. It's going to be pulled down to make way for a supermarket. You know it has a king-pin roof, don't you?"

25

"Oh," said Charles. "Has it?"

"And a queen-pin," said Miss Cadwallader.

Charles seemed to have got saddled with the conversation. Nirupam was happy enough not to talk, and Nan dared do no more than nod intelligently, in case she started describing the food again. As Miss Cadwallader talked, and Charles was forced to answer while trying to eat tinned tomatoes – no, they were *not* skinned mice! – using just a fork, Charles began to feel he was undergoing a particularly refined form of torture. He realized he needed a hate-word for Miss Cadwallader too. Hot-pot would do for her. Surely nothing as awful as this could happen to him more than once a month? But that meant he had still not got a code-word for Nan.

They took the hot-pot away. Charles had not eaten much. Miss Cadwallader continued to talk to him about houses in the town, then about stately homes in the country, until the pudding arrived. It was set before Charles, white and bleak and swimming, with little white grains in it like the corpses of ants – Lord, he was getting as bad as Nan Pilgrim! Then he realized it was the ideal word for Nan.

"Rice pudding!" he exclaimed.

"It *is* agreeable," Miss Cadwallader said, smiling. "And so nourishing." Then, incredibly, she reached to the top of her plate and picked up a fork. Charles stared. He waited. Surely Miss Cadwallader was not going to eat runny rice pudding with just a fork? But she was. She dipped the fork in and brought it up, raining weak white milk.

Slowly, Charles picked up a fork too and turned to meet Nan's and Nirupam's incredulous faces. It was just not possible.

Nirupam looked wretchedly down at his brimming plate. "There is a story in the *Arabian Nights*," he said, "about a woman who ate rice with a pin, grain by grain." Charles shot a terrified look at Miss Cadwallader, but she was talking to the lord again. "She turned out to be a ghoul," Nirupam said. "She ate her fill of corpses every night."

Charles's terrified look shot to Nan instead. "Shut up, you fool! You'll set her off again!"

But the possession seemed to have left Nan by then. She was able to whisper, with her head bent over her plate so that only the boys could hear, "Mr Wentworth's using his spoon. Look."

"Do you think we dare?" said Nirupam.

"I'm going to," said Charles. "I'm hungry."

So they all used their spoons. When the meal was at last over, they were all dismayed to find Mr Wentworth beckoning. But it was only Nan he was beckoning. When she came reluctantly over, he said, "See me at four in my study." Which was, Nan felt, all she needed. And the day was still only half over.

Chapter Three

That afternoon, Nan came into the classroom to find a besom laid across her desk. It was an old tatty broom, with only the bare minimum of twigs left in the brush end, which the groundsman sometimes used to sweep the paths. Someone had brought it in from the groundsman's shed. Someone had tied a label to the handle: *Dulcinea's Pony*. Nan recognized the round, angelic writing as Theresa's.

Amid sniggers and titters, she looked round the assembled faces. Theresa would not have thought of stealing a broom on her own. Estelle? No. Neither Estelle nor Karen Grigg was there. No, it was Dan Smith, by the look on his face. Then she looked at Simon Silverson and was not so sure. It could not have been both of them because they never, ever did anything together.

Simon said to her, in his suavest manner, grinning all over his face, "Why don't you hop on and have a ride, Dulcinea?"

"Yes, go on. Ride it, Dulcinea," said Dan.

Next moment, everyone else was laughing and yelling at her to ride the broom. And Brian Wentworth, who was only too ready to torment other people when he was not being a victim himself, was leaping up and down in the gangway between the desks, screaming, "Ride, Dulcinea! Ride!"

Slowly, Nan picked up the broom. She was a mild and peaceable person who seldom lost her temper – perhaps that was her trouble – but when she did lose it, there was no knowing what she would do. As she picked up the broom, she thought she just meant to stand it haughtily against the wall. But, as her hands closed round its knobby handle, her temper left her completely. She turned round on the jeering, hooting crowd, filled with roaring rage. She lifted the broom high above her head and bared her teeth. Everyone thought that was funnier than ever.

Nan meant to smash the broom through Simon Silverson's laughing face. She meant to bash in Dan Smith's head. But, since Brian Wentworth was dancing and shrieking and making faces just in front of her, it was Brian she went for. Luckily for him, he saw the broom coming down and leapt clear. After that, he was forced to back away up the gangway and then into the space by the door, with his arms over his head, screaming for mercy, while Nan followed him, bashing like a madwoman.

"Help! Stop her!" Brian screamed, and backed into the door just as Miss Hodge came through it carrying a large pile of English books. Brian backed into her and sat down at her feet in a shower of books. "Ow!" he yelled.

"What is going on?" said Miss Hodge.

The uproar in the room was cut off as if with a switch. "Get up, Brian," Simon Silverson said righteously. "It was your own fault for teasing Nan Pilgrim."

"Really! Nan!" said Theresa. She was genuinely shocked. "Temper, temper!"

At that, Nan nearly went for Theresa with the broom. Theresa was only saved by the fortunate arrival of Estelle Green and Karen Grigg. They came scurrying in with their heads guiltily lowered and their arms wrapped round bulky bags of knitting wool. "Sorry we're late, Miss Hodge," Estelle panted. "We had permission to go shopping."

Nan's attention was distracted. The wool in the bags was fluffy and white, just like Theresa's. Why on earth,

29

Nan wondered scornfully, did everyone have to imitate Theresa?

Miss Hodge took the broom out of Nan's unresisting hands and propped it neatly behind the door. "Sit down, all of you," she said. She was very put out. She had intended to come quietly in to a nice quiet classroom and galvanize 2Y by confronting them with her scheme. And here they were galvanized already, *and* with a witch's broom. There was clearly no chance of catching the writer of the note or the witch by surprise. Still, she did not like to let a good scheme go to waste.

"I thought we would have a change today," she said, when everyone was settled. "Our poetry book doesn't seem to be going down very well, does it?" She looked brightly round the class. 2Y looked back cautiously. Some of them felt anything would be better than being asked to find poems beautiful. Some of them felt it depended on what Miss Hodge intended to do instead. Of the rest, Nan was trying not to cry, Brian was licking a scratch on his arm, and Charles was glowering. Charles liked poetry because the lines were so short. You could think your own thoughts in the spaces round the print.

"Today," said Miss Hodge, "I want you all to do something yourselves."

Everyone recoiled. Estelle put her hand up. "Please, Miss Hodge. I don't know how to write poems."

"Oh, I don't want you to do that," said Miss Hodge. Everyone relaxed. "I want you to act out some little plays for me." Everyone recoiled again. Miss Hodge took no notice and explained that she was going to call them out to the front in pairs, a boy and a girl in each, and every pair was going to act out the same short scene. "That way," she said, "we shall have fifteen different pocket dramas." By this time, most of 2Y were staring at her in wordless despair. Miss Hodge smiled warmly and prepared to galvanize them. Really, she thought, her scheme might go quite well after all. "Now, we must choose a subject for our playlets. It has to be something strong and striking, with passionate possibilities. Suppose we act a pair of lovers saying good-bye?" Somebody groaned, as Miss Hodge had known somebody would. "Very well. Who has a suggestion?"

Theresa's hand was up, and Dan Smith's.

"A television star and her admirer," said Theresa.

"A murderer and a policeman making him confess," said Dan. "Are we allowed torture?"

"No, we are not," said Miss Hodge, at which Dan lost interest. "Anyone else?"

Nirupam raised a long thin arm. "A salesman deceiving a lady over a car."

Well, Miss Hodge thought, she had not really expected anyone to make a suggestion that would give them away. She pretended to consider. "We-ell, so far the most dramatic suggestion is Dan's. But I had in mind something really tense, which we all know about quite well."

"We all know about murder," Dan protested.

"Yes," said Miss Hodge. She was watching everyone like a hawk now. "But we know even more about stealing, say, or lying, or witchcraft, or—" She let herself notice the broomstick again, with a start of surprise. It came in handy after all. "I know! Let us suppose that one of the people in our little play is suspected of being a witch, and the other is an Inquisitor. How about that?"

Nothing. Not a soul in 2Y reacted, except Dan. "That's the same as my idea," he grumbled. "And it's no fun without torture."

Miss Hodge made Dan into suspect number one at once. "Then you begin, Dan," she said, "with Theresa. Which are you, Theresa — witch or Inquisitor?"

"Inquisitor, Miss Hodge," Theresa said promptly.

"It's not fair!" said Dan. "I don't know what witches do!"

31

Nor did he, it was clear. And it was equally clear that Theresa had no more idea what Inquisitors did. They stood woodenly by the blackboard. Dan stared at the ceiling, while Theresa stated, "You are a witch." Whereupon Dan told the ceiling, "No I am not." And they went on doing this until Miss Hodge told them to stop. Regretfully, she demoted Dan from first suspect to last, and put Theresa down there with him, and called up the next pair.

Nobody behaved suspiciously. Most people's idea was to get the acting over as quickly as possible. Some argued a little, for the look of the thing. Others tried running about to make things seem dramatic. And first prize for brevity certainly went to Simon Silverson and Karen Grigg. Simon said, "I know you're a witch, so don't argue."

And Karen replied, "Yes I am. I give in. Let's stop now."

By the time it came to Nirupam, Miss Hodge's list of suspects was all bottom and no top. Then Nirupam put on a terrifying performance as Inquisitor. His eyes blazed. His voice alternately roared and fell to a sinister whisper. He pointed fiercely at Estelle's face. "Look at your evil eyes!" he bellowed. Then he whispered, "I see you, I feel you, I know you — you *are* a witch!" Estelle was so frightened that she gave a real performance of terrified innocence. But Brian Wentworth's performance as a witch outshone even Nirupam. Brian wept, he cringed, he made obviously false excuses, and he ended kneeling at Delia Martin's feet, sobbing for mercy and crying real tears.

Everyone was astonished, including Miss Hodge. She would dearly have liked to put Brian at the top of her list of suspects, either as the witch or the one who wrote the note. But how bothersome for her plans if she had to go to Mr Wentworth and say it was Brian. No, she decided. There was no genuine feeling in Brian's performance, and the same went for Nirupam. They were both just good actors.

Then it was the turn of Charles and Nan. Charles had seen it coming for some time now, that he would be paired with Nan. He was very annoyed. He seemed to be haunted by her today. But he did not intend to let that stop his performance being a triumph of comic acting. He was depressed by the lack of invention everyone except Nirupam had shown. Nobody had thought of making the Inquisitor funny. "I'll be Inquisitor," he said quickly.

But Nan was still smarting after the broomstick. She thought Charles was getting at her and glared at him. Charles, on principle, never let anyone glare at him without giving his nastiest double-barrelled stare in return. So they shuffled to the front of the class looking daggers at one another.

There Charles beat at his forehead. "Emergency!" he exclaimed. "There are no witches for the autumn bonefires. I shall have to find an ordinary person instead." He pointed at Nan. "You'll do," he said. "Starting from now, you're a witch."

Nan had not realized that the acting had begun. Besides, she was too hurt and angry to care. "Oh, no I'm not!" she snapped. "Why shouldn't you be the witch?"

"Because I can prove you're a witch," Charles said, trying to stick to his part. "Being an Inquisitor, I can prove anything."

"In that case," said Nan, angrily ignoring this fine acting, "we'll both be Inquisitors, and I'll prove you're a witch too! Why not? You have four of the most evil eyes I ever saw. And your feet smell."

All eyes turned to Charles's feet. Since he had been forced to run round the field in the shoes he was wearing now, they were still rather wet. And, being warmed through, they were indeed exuding a slight but definite smell.

"Cheese," murmured Simon Silverson.

Charles looked angrily down at his shoes. Nan had reminded him that he was in trouble over his missing running-shoes. And she had spoilt his acting. He hated her. He was in an ecstasy of hate again. "Worms and custard and dead mice!" he said. Everyone stared at him, mystified. "Tinned peas soaked in sewage!" Charles said, beside himself with hatred. "Potatoes in scum. I'm not surprised your name's Dulcinea. It suits you. You're quite disgusting!"

"And so are you!" Nan shouted back at him. "I bet it was you who did those birds in Music yesterday!" This caused shocked gasps from the rest of 2Y.

Miss Hodge listened, fascinated. This was real feeling all right. And *what* had Charles said? It was clear to her now why the rest of 2Y had clustered so depressingly at the bottom of her list of suspects. Nan and Charles were at the top of it. It was obvious. They were always the odd ones out in 2Y. Nan must have written the note, and Charles must be the witch in question. And now let Mr Wentworth pour scorn on her scheme!

"Please, Miss Hodge, the bell's gone," called a number of voices.

The door opened and Mr Crossley came in. When he saw Miss Hodge, which he had come early in order to do, his face became a deep red, most interesting to Estelle and Theresa. "Am I interrupting a lesson, Miss Hodge?"

"Not at all," said Miss Hodge. "We had just finished. Nan and Charles go back to your places." And she swept out of the room, without appearing to notice that Mr Crossley had leapt to hold the door open for her.

Miss Hodge hurried straight upstairs to Mr Wentworth's study. She knew this news was going to make an impression on him. But there, to her annoyance, was Mr Wentworth dashing downstairs with a box of chalk, very late for a lesson with 3Z.

"Oh, Mr Wentworth," panted Miss Hodge. "Can you

spare a moment?"

"Not a second. Write me a memo if it's urgent," said Mr Wentworth, dashing on down.

Miss Hodge reached out and seized his arm. "But you must! You know 2Y and my scheme about the anonymous note—"

Mr Wentworth swung round on the end of her clutching hands and looked up at her irritably. "What about what anonymous note?"

"My scheme worked!" Miss Hodge said. "Nan Pilgrim wrote it, I'm sure. You must see her—"

"I'm seeing her at four o'clock," said Mr Wentworth. "If you think I need to know, write me a memo, Miss Hodge."

"Eileen," said Miss Hodge.

"Eileen who?" said Mr Wentworth, trying to pull his arm away. "You mean two girls wrote this note?"

"My name is Eileen," said Miss Hodge, hanging on.

"Miss Hodge," said Mr Wentworth, "3Z will be breaking windows by now!"

"But there's Charles Morgan too!" Miss Hodge cried out, feeling his arm pulling out of her hands. "Mr Wentworth, I swear that boy recited a spell! Worms and custard and scummy potatoes, he said. All sorts of nasty things."

Mr Wentworth succeeded in tearing his arm loose and set off downstairs again. His voice came back to Miss Hodge. "Slugs and snails and puppy-dogs' tails. Write it all down, Miss Hodge."

"Bother!" said Miss Hodge. "But I *will* write it down. He *is* going to notice!" She went at once to the staff room, where she spent the rest of the lesson composing an account of her experiment, in writing almost as round and angelic as Theresa's.

Meanwhile, in the 2Y classroom, Mr Crossley shut the door behind Miss Hodge with a sigh. "Journals out," he said. He had come to a decision about the note, and

35

he did not intend to let his feelings about Miss Hodge interfere with his duty. So, before anyone could start writing in a journal and make it impossible for him to interrupt, he made 2Y a long and serious speech. He told them how malicious and sneaky and unkind it was to write anonymous accusations. He asked them to consider how they would feel if someone had written a note about them. Then he told them that someone in 2Y had written just such a note.

"I'm not going to tell you what was in it," he said. "I shall only say it accused someone of a very serious crime. I want you all to think about it while you write your journals, and after you've finished, I want the person who wrote the note to write me another note confessing who they are and why they wrote it. That's all. I shan't punish the person. I just want them to see what a serious thing they have done."

Having said this, Mr Crossley sat back to do some marking, feeling he had settled the matter in a most understanding way. In front of him, 2Y picked up their pens. Thanks to Miss Hodge, everyone thought they knew exactly what Mr Crossley meant.

29 October, wrote Theresa. *There is a witch in our class. Mr Crossley just said so. He wants the witch to confess. Mr Wentworth confiscated my knitting this morning and made jokes about it. I did not get it back till lunchtime. Estelle Green has started knitting now. What a copycat that girl is. Nan Pilgrim couldn't climb the ropes this morning and her name is Dulcinea. That made us laugh a lot.*

29.10.81. Mr Crossley has just talked to us very seriously, Simon Silverson wrote, very seriously, *about a guilty person in our class. I shall do my best to bring that person to justice. If we don't catch them we might all be accused. This is off the record of course.*

Nan Pilgrim is a witch, Dan Smith wrote. *This is not a private thought because Mr Crossley just told us. I think*

36

she is a witch too. She is even called after that famous witch, but I can't spell it. I hope they burn her where we can see.

Mr Crossley has been talking about serious accusations, Estelle wrote. *And Miss Hodge has been making us all accuse one another. It was quite frightening. I hope none of it is true. Poor Teddy went awfully red when he saw Miss Hodge but she scorned him again.*

While everyone else was writing the same sort of things, there were four people in the class who were writing something quite different.

Nirupam wrote, *Today, no comment. I shall not even think about high table.*

Brian Wentworth, oblivious to everything, scribbled down how he would get from Timbuktu to Uttar Pradesh by bus, allowing time for roadworks on Sundays.

Nan sat for a considerable while wondering what to write. She wanted desperately to get some of today off her chest, but she could not at first think how to do it without saying something personal. At last she wrote, in burning indignation, *I do not know if 2Y is average or not, but this is how they are. They are divided into girls and boys with an invisible line down the middle of the room and people only cross that line when teachers make them. Girls are divided into real girls (Theresa Mullett) and imitations (Estelle Green). And me. Boys are divided into real boys (Simon Silverson), brutes (Daniel Smith) and unreal boys (Nirupam Singh). And Charles Morgan. And Brian Wentworth. What makes you a real girl or boy is that no one laughs at you. If you are imitation or unreal, the rules give you a right to exist provided you do what the real ones or brutes say. What makes you into me or Charles Morgan is that the rules allow all the girls to be better than me and all the boys better than Charles Morgan. They are allowed to cross the invisible line to prove this. Everyone is allowed to cross the invisible line to be nasty to Brian Wentworth.*

Nan paused here. Up to then she been writing almost as if she was possessed, the way she had been at lunch. Now she had to think about Brian Wentworth. What was it about Brian that put him below even her? *Some of Brian's trouble,* she wrote, *is that Mr Wentworth is his father, and he is small and perky and irritating with it. Another part is that Brian is really good at things and comes top in most things, and he ought to be the real boy, not Simon. But SS is so certain he is the real boy that he has managed to convince Brian too.* That, Nan thought, was still not quite it, but it was as near as she could get. The rest of her description of 2Y struck her as masterly. She was so pleased with it that she almost forgot she was miserable.

Charles wrote, *I got up, I got up, I GOT UP.* That made it look as if he had sprung eagerly out of bed, which was certainly not the case, but he had so hated today that he had to work it off somehow. *My running-shoes got buried in cornflakes. I felt very hot running round the field and on top of that I had lunch on high table. I do not like rice pudding. We have had Games with Miss Hodge and rice pudding and there are still about a hundred years of today still to go.* And that, he thought, about summed it up.

When the bell went, Mr Crossley hurried to pick up the books he had been marking in order to get to the staff room before Miss Hodge left it. And stared. There was another note under the pile of books. It was written in the same capitals and the same blue ballpoint as the first note. It said: *HA HA. THOUGHT I WAS GOING TO TELL YOU. DIDN'T YOU?*

Now what do I do? wondered Mr Crossley.

Chapter Four

At the end of lessons, there was the usual stampede to be elsewhere. Theresa and her friends, Delia, Heather, Deborah, Julia and the rest, raced to the lower school girls' playroom to bag the radiators there, so that they could sit on them and knit. Estelle and Karen hurried to bag the chillier radiators in the corridor, and sat on them to cast on their stitches. Simon led his friends to the labs, where they added to Simon's collection of honour marks by helping tidy up. Dan Smith left his friends to play football without him, because he had business in the shrubbery, watching the senior boys meeting their senior girlfriends there. Charles crawled reluctantly to the locker room to look for his running shoes again. Nan went, equally reluctantly, up to Mr Wentworth's study.

There was someone else in with Mr Wentworth when she got there. She could hear voices and see two misty shapes through the wobbly glass in the door. Nan did not mind. The longer the interview was put off the better. So she hung about in the passage for nearly twenty minutes, until a passing prefect asked her what she was doing there.

"Waiting to see Mr Wentworth," Nan said. Then, of course, in order to prove it to the prefect, she was forced to knock at the door.

"Come!" bawled Mr Wentworth.

The prefect, placated, passed on down the passage. Nan put out her hand to open the door, but, before she could, it was pulled open by Mr Wentworth himself and

Mr Crossley came out, rather red and laughing sheepishly.

"I still swear it wasn't there when I put the books down," he said.

"Ah, but you know you didn't look, Harold," Mr Wentworth said. "Our practical joker relied on your not looking. Forget it, Harold. So there you are, Nan. Did you lose your way here? Come on in. Mr Crossley's just going."

He went back to his desk and sat down. Mr Crossley hovered for a moment, still rather red, and then hurried away downstairs, leaving Nan to shut the door. As she did so, she noticed that Mr Wentworth was staring at three pieces of paper on his desk as if he thought they might bite him. She saw that one was in Miss Hodge's writing and that the other two were scraps of paper with blue capital letters on them, but she was much too worried on her own account to bother about pieces of writing.

"Explain your behaviour on high table," Mr Wentworth said to her.

Since there really was no explanation that Nan could see, she said, in a miserable whisper, "I can't, sir," and looked down at the parquet floor.

"Can't?" said Mr Wentworth. "You put Lord Mulke off his lunch for no reason at all! Tell me another. Explain yourself."

Miserably, Nan fitted one of her feet exactly into one of the parquet oblongs in the floor. "I don't know, sir. I just said it."

"You don't know, you just said it," said Mr Wentworth. "Do you mean by that you found yourself speaking without knowing you were?"

This was meant to be sarcasm, Nan knew. But it seemed to be true as well. Carefully, she fitted her other shoe into the parquet block which slanted towards her first foot, and stood unsteadily, toe to toe, while she

40

wondered how to explain. "I didn't know what I was going to say next, sir."

"Why not?" demanded Mr Wentworth.

"I don't know," Nan said. "It was like – like being possessed."

"*Possessed!*" shouted Mr Wentworth. It was the way he shouted just before he suddenly threw chalk at people. Nan went backwards to avoid the chalk which came next. But she forgot that her feet were pointing inwards and sat down heavily on the floor. From there, she could see Mr Wentworth's surprised face, peering at her over the top of his desk. "What did that?" he said.

"Please don't throw chalk at me!" Nan said.

At that moment, there was a knock at the door and Brian Wentworth put his head round it into the room. "Are you free yet, Dad?"

"No," said Mr Wentworth.

Both of them looked at Nan sitting on the floor. "What's she doing?" Brian asked.

"She says she's possessed. Go away and come back in ten minutes," Mr Wentworth said. "Get up, Nan."

Brian obediently shut the door and went away. Nan struggled to her feet. It was almost as difficult as climbing a rope. She wondered a little how it felt to be Brian, with your father one of the teachers, but mostly she wondered what Mr Wentworth was going to do to her. He had his most harrowed, worried look, and he was staring again at the three papers on his desk.

"So you think you're possessed?" he said.

"Oh no," Nan said. "All I meant was it was *like* it. I knew I was going to do something awful before I started, but I didn't know what until I started describing the food. Then I tried to stop and I couldn't, somehow."

"Do you often get taken that way?" Mr Wentworth asked.

Nan was about to answer indignantly No, when she realized that she had gone for Brian with the witch's

41

broom in exactly the same way straight after lunch. And many and many a time, she had impulsively written things in her journal. She fitted her shoe into a parquet block again, and hastily took it away. "Sometimes," she said, in a low, guilty mutter. "I do sometimes – when I'm angry with people – I write what I think in my journal."

"And do you write notes to teachers too?" asked Mr Wentworth.

"Of course not," said Nan. "What would be the point?"

"But someone in 2Y has written Mr Crossley a note," said Mr Wentworth. "It accused someone in the class of being a witch."

The serious, worried way he said it made Nan understand at last. So that was why Mr Crossley had talked like that and then been to see Mr Wentworth. And they thought Nan had written the note. "The unfairness!" she burst out. "How *can* they think I wrote the note *and* call me a witch too! Just because my name's Dulcinea!"

"You could be diverting suspicion from yourself," Mr Wentworth pointed out. "If I asked you straight out —"

"I am *not* a witch!" said Nan. "And I didn't write that note. I bet that was Theresa Mullett or Simon Silverson. They're both born accusers! Or Daniel Smith," she added.

"Now I wouldn't have picked on Dan," Mr Wentworth said. "I wasn't aware he could write."

The sarcastic way he said that showed Nan that she ought not to have mentioned Theresa or Simon. Like everyone else, Mr Wentworth thought of them as the real girl and the real boy. "Someone accused *me*," she said bitterly.

"Well, I'll take your word for it that you didn't write the note," Mr Wentworth said. "And next time you feel a possession coming on, take a deep breath and count up to ten, or you may be in serious trouble. You have a very unfortunate name, you see. You'll have to be very careful in future. How did you come to be called Dulcinea? Were you called after the Archwitch?"

"Yes," Nan admitted. "I'm descended from her."

Mr Wentworth whistled. "And you're a witch-orphan too, aren't you? I shouldn't let anyone else know that, if I were you. I happen to admire Dulcinea Wilkes for trying to stop witches being persecuted, but very few other people do. Keep your mouth shut, Nan — and don't ever describe food in front of Lord Mulke again either. Off you go now."

Nan fumbled her way out of the study and plunged down the stairs. Her eyes were so fuzzy with indignation that she could hardly see where she was going. "What does he take me for?" she muttered to herself as she went. "I'd rather admit to being descended from — from Attila the Hun or — or Guy Fawkes. Or anyone."

It was around that time that Mr Towers, who had stood over Charles while Charles hunted unavailingly for his running-shoes in the boys' locker room, finally smothered a long yawn and left Charles to go on looking by himself. "Bring them to me in the staff room when you've found them," he said.

Charles sat down on a bench, alone among grey lockers and green walls. He glowered at the slimy grey floor and the three odd football boots that always lay in one corner. He looked at nameless garments withering on pegs. He sniffed the smell of sweat and old socks. "I hate everything," he said. He had searched everywhere. Dan Smith had found a really cunning place for those shoes. The only way Charles was going to find them was by Dan telling him where they were.

Charles ground his teeth and stood up. "All right. Then I'll ask him," he said. Like everyone else, he knew Dan was in the shrubbery spying on seniors. Dan made no secret of it. He had got his uncle to send him a pair of binoculars so that he could get a really close view. And the shrubbery was only round the corner from the locker room. Charles thought he could risk going there, even if Mr Towers suddenly came back. The real risk was from the seniors in the shrubbery. There was an invisible line round the shrubbery, just like the one Nan had described between the boys and the girls in 2Y. Anyone younger than a senior who got found in the shrubbery could be most thoroughly beaten up by the senior who found them. Still, Charles thought, as he set off, Dan was not a senior either. That should help.

The shrubbery was a messy tangle of huge evergreen bushes, with wet grass in between. Charles's almost-dry shoes were soaked again before he found Dan. He found him quite quickly. Since it was a cold evening and the grass was so wet, there were only two pairs of seniors there, and they were all in the most trodden part, on either side of a mighty laurel bush. Ah! thought Charles. He crept to the laurel bush and pushed his face in among the wet and shiny leaves. Dan was there, among the dry branches inside.

"Dan!" hissed Charles.

Dan took his binoculars from his eyes with a jerk and whirled round. When he saw Charles's face leaning in among the leaves at him, beaming its nastiest double-barrelled glare, he seemed almost relieved. "Pig off!" he whispered. "Magic out of here!"

"What have you done with my spikes?" said Charles.

"Whisper, can't you?" Dan whispered. He peered nervously through the leaves at the nearest pair of seniors. Charles could see them too. They were a tall thin boy and a very fat girl – much fatter than Nan Pilgrim – and they did not seem to have heard anything. Charles could see the thin boy's fingers digging into the girl's fat where his arm was round her. He wondered how anyone could enjoy grabbing, or watching, such fatness.

"Where have you hidden my spikes?" he whispered.

But Dan did not care, as long as the seniors had not heard. "I've forgotten," he whispered. Beyond the bush, the thin boy leant his head against the fat girl's head. Dan grinned. "See that? Mixing the breed." He put his binoculars to his eyes again.

Charles spoke a little louder. "Tell me where you've put my spikes, or I'll shout that you're here."

"Then they'll know you're here then too, won't they?" Dan whispered. "I told you, magic off!"

"Not till you tell me," said Charles.

Dan turned his back on Charles. "You're boring me."

Charles saw that he had no option but to raise a yell and fetch the seniors into the bush. While he was wondering whether he dared, the second pair of seniors came hurrying round the laurel bush. "Hey!" said the boy. "There's some juniors in that bush. Sue heard them whispering."

"Right!" said the thin boy and the fat girl. And all four seniors dived at the bush.

Charles let out a squawk of terror and ran. Behind him, he heard cracking branches, leaves swishing, grunts, crunchings, and most unladylike threats from the senior girls. He hoped Dan had been caught. But even while he was hoping, he knew Dan had got away. Charles was in the open. The seniors had seen him and it was Charles they were after. He burst out of the shrubbery with all four of them after him. With a finger across his nose to hold his glasses on, he pelted for his life round the corner of the school.

There was nothing in front of him but a long wall and open space. The lower school door was a hundred yards away. The only possible place that was any nearer was the open door of the boys' locker room. Charles bolted through it without thinking. And skidded to a stop, realizing what a fool he had been. The seniors' feet were hammering round the corner, and the only way out of the locker room was the open door he had come in by. All Charles could think of was to dodge behind that door and stand there flat against the wall, hoping. There

45

he stood, flattened and desperate, breathing in old sock and mildew and trying not to pant, while four pairs of feet slid to a stop outside the door.

"He's hiding in there," said the fat girl's voice.

"We can't go in. It's boys'," said the other girl. "You two go and bring him out."

There were breathless grunts from the two boys, and two pairs of heavy feet tramped in through the doorway. The thin boy, by the sound, tramped into the middle of the room. His voice rumbled round the concrete space.

"Where's he got to?"

"Must be behind the door," rumbled the other. The door was pulled aside. Charles stood petrified at the sight of the senior it revealed. This one was huge. He towered over Charles. He even had a sort of moustache. Charles shook with terror.

But the little angry eyes, high up above the moustache, stared down through Charles, seemingly at the floor and the wall. The bulky face twitched in annoyance. "Nope," said the senior. "Nothing here."

"He must have made it to the lower school door," said the thin boy.

"Magicking little witch!" said the other.

And, to Charles's utter amazement, the two of them tramped out of the locker room. There was some annoyed exclaiming from the two girls outside, and then all four of them seemed to be going away. Charles stood where he was, shaking, for quite a while after they seemed to have gone. He was sure it was a trick. But, five minutes later, they had still not come back. It was a miracle of some kind!

Charles tottered out into the middle of the room, wondering just what kind of miracle it was that could make a huge senior look straight through you. Now he knew it had happened, Charles was sure the senior had not been pretending. He really had not seen Charles standing there.

"So what did it?" Charles asked the nameless hanging clothes. "Magic?"

He meant it to be a scornful question, the kind of thing you say when you give the whole thing up. But, somehow, it was not. As he said it, a huge, terrible suspicion which had been gathering, almost unnoticed, at the back of Charles's head, like a headache coming on, now swung to the front of his mind, like a headache already there. Charles began shaking again.

"No," he said. "It wasn't that. It was something else!"

But the suspicion, now it was there, demanded to be sent away at once, now, completely. "All right," Charles said. "I'll prove it. I know how. I hate Dan Smith anyway."

He marched up to Dan's locker and opened it. He looked at the jumble of clothes and shoes inside. He had searched this locker twice now. He had searched all of them twice. He was sick of looking in lockers. He took up Dan's spiked running shoes, one in each hand, and backed away with them to the middle of the room.

"Now," he said to the shoes, "you vanish." He tapped them together, sole to spiked sole, to make it clear to them. "Vanish," he said. "Abracadabra." And, when nothing happened, he threw both shoes into the air, to give them every chance. "Hey presto," he said.

Both shoes were gone, in mid-air, before they reached the slimy floor.

Charles stared at the spot where he had last seen them. "I didn't mean it," he said hopelessly. "Come back."

Nothing happened. No shoes appeared.

"Oh well," said Charles. "Perhaps I did mean it."

Then, very gently, almost reverently, he went over and shut Dan's locker. The suspicion was gone. But the certainty which hung over Charles in its place was so heavy and so hideous that it made him want to crouch on the floor. He was a witch. He would be hunted like the witch he had helped and burnt like the fat one. It would hurt. It

47

would be horrible. He was very, very scared – so scared it was like being dead already, cold, heavy and almost unable to breathe.

Trying to pull himself together, he took his glasses off to clean them. That made him notice that he was, actually, crouching on the floor beside Dan's locker. He dragged himself upright. What should he do? Might not the best thing be to get it over now, and go straight to Miss Cadwallader and confess?

That seemed an awful waste, but Charles could not seem to think of anything else to do. He shuffled to the door and out into the chilly evening. He had always known he was wicked, he thought. Now it was proved. The witch had kissed him because she had known he was evil too. Now he had grown so evil that he needed to be stamped out. He wouldn't give the Inquisitors any trouble, not like some witches did. Witchcraft must show all over him anyway. Someone had already noticed and written that note about it. Nan Pilgrim had accused him of conjuring up all those birds in Music yesterday. Charles thought he must have done that without knowing he had, just as he had made himself invisible to the seniors just now. He wondered how strong a witch he was. Were you more wicked, the stronger you were? Probably. But weak or powerful, you were burned just the same. And he was in nice time for the autumn bone-fires. It was nearly Hallowe'en now. By the time they had legally proved him a witch, it would be 5 November, and that would be the end of it.

He did not know it was possible to feel so scared and hopeless.

Thinking and thinking, in a haze of horror, Charles shuffled his way to Miss Cadwallader's room. He stood outside the door and waited, without even the heart to knock. Minutes passed. The door opened. Seeing the misty oblong of bright light, Charles braced himself.

"So you didn't find them?" said Mr Towers.

Charles jumped. Though he could not see what Mr Towers was doing here, he said, "No, sir."

"I'm not surprised, if you took your glasses off to look," said Mr Towers.

Tremulously, Charles hooked his glasses over his ears. They were ice-cold. He must have had them in his hand ever since he took them off to clean. Now he could see, he saw he was standing outside the staff room, not Miss Cadwallader's room at all. Why was that? Still he could just as easily confess to Mr Towers. "Please, I deserve to be punished, sir. I —"

"Take a black mark for that," Mr Towers said coldly. "I don't like boys who crawl. Now, either you can pay for a new pair of shoes, or you can write five hundred lines every night until the end of term. Come to me tomorrow morning and tell me which you decide to do. Now get out of here."

He slammed the door of the staff room in Charles's face. Charles stood and looked at it. That was a fierce choice Mr Towers had given him. And a black mark. But it had jolted his horror off sideways somehow. He felt his face going red. What a fool he was! Nobody knew he was a witch. Instinct had told him this, and taken his feet to the staff room instead of to Miss Cadwallader. But only luck had saved him confessing to Mr Towers. He had better not be that stupid again. As long as he kept his mouth shut and worked no more magic, he would be perfectly safe. He almost smiled as he trudged off to supper.

But he could not stop thinking about it. Round and round and round, all through supper. How wicked was he? Could he do anything about it? Was it enough just not to do any magic? Could you go somewhere and be de-magicked, like clothes were dry-cleaned? If not, and he was found out, was it any use running away? Where did witches run to, after they had run through people's back-gardens? Was there any certain way of being safe?

49

"Oh magic!" someone exclaimed, just beside him. "I left my book in the playroom!" Charles jumped and hummed, like the school gong when it was hit, at the mere word.

"Don't swear," said the prefect in charge.

Then Theresa Mullett, from the end of the table, called out in a way that was not quite jeering, "Nan, won't you do something interesting and miraculous for us? We know you can." Charles jumped and hummed again.

"No I can't," said Nan.

But Theresa, and Delia Martin too, kept on asking. "Nan, high table's got some lovely bananas. Won't you say a spell and fetch them over?"

"Nan, I feel like some ice-cream. Conjure some up."

"Nan, do you really worship the devil?"

Each time they said any of these things, Charles jumped and hummed. Though he knew it was entirely to his advantage to have everyone think Nan Pilgrim was the witch, he wanted to scream at the girls to stop. He was very relieved, halfway through supper, when Nan jumped up and stormed out of the dining room.

Nan went straight to the deserted library. Very well, she thought. If everyone was so sure she was guilty, she could at least take advantage of it and do something she had always wanted to do and never dared to do before. She took down the encyclopaedia and looked up Dulcinea Wilkes. Curiously enough, the fat book fell open at that page. It seemed as if a lot of people at Larwood House had taken an interest in the Archwitch. If so, they had all been as disappointed as Nan. The laws against witchcraft were so severe that most information about Nan's famous ancestress was banned. The entry was quite short.

WILKES, DULCINEA. 1760–1790. Notorious witch, known as the Archwitch. Born in Steeple

Bumpstead, Essex, she moved to London in 1781, where she soon became well known for her nightly broomstick flights round St Paul's and the Houses of Parliament. Besoms are still sometimes called "Dulcinea's Ponies". Dulcinea took a leading part in the Witches' Uprising of 1789. She was arrested and burnt, along with the other leaders. While she was burning, it is said that the lead on the roof of St Paul's melted and ran off the dome. She continued to be burnt in effigy every bone-fire day until 1845, when the practice was discontinued owing to the high price of lead.

Nan sighed and put the encyclopaedia back. When the bell rang, she went slowly to the classroom to do the work that had been set during the day. It was called devvy at Larwood House, no one knew why. Everyone else was there when Nan arrived. The room was full of the slap of exercise books round Brian Wentworth's head and Brian squealing. But the noise stopped as Nan came in, showing that Mr Crossley had come in behind her.

"Charles Morgan," said Mr Crossley. "Mr Wentworth wants to see you."

Charles dragged his mind with a jolt from imaginary flames whirling round him. He got up and trudged off, like a boy in a dream, along corridors and through swing doors to the part of the school where teachers who lived in the school had their private rooms. He had only been to Mr Wentworth's room once before. He had to tear his mind away from thoughts of burning and look at the names on the doors. He supposed Mr Wentworth wanted him because of his beastly shoes. Blast and magic Dan Smith! He knocked on the door.

"Come!" said Mr Wentworth.

He was sitting in an armchair smoking a pipe. The room was full of strong smoke. Charles was surprised to see how shabby Mr Wentworth's room was. The armchair was worn out. There were holes in the soles of Mr Wentworth's slippers, and holes in the hearthrug the slippers rested on. But the gas-fire was churring away comfortably and the room was beautifully warm compared with the rest of school.

"Ah, Charles." Mr Wentworth laid his pipe in an ashtray that looked like Brian's first attempt at pottery. "Charles, I was told this afternoon that you might be a witch."

Chapter Five

Charles had thought, in the locker room, that he had been as frightened as a person could possibly be. Now he discovered this was not so. Mr Wentworth's words seemed to hit him heavy separate blows. Under the blows, Charles felt as if he were dissolving and falling away somewhere far, far below. He thought at first he was falling somewhere so sickeningly deep that the whole of his mind had become one long horrible scream. Then he felt he was rising up as he screamed. The shabby room was blurred and swaying, but Charles could have sworn he was now looking down on it from somewhere near the ceiling. He seemed to be hanging there, screaming, looking down on the top of his own head, and the slightly bald top of Mr Wentworth's head, and the smoke writhing from the pipe in the ashtray. And that terrified him too. He must have divided into two parts. Mr Wentworth was bound to notice.

To his surprise, the part of himself left standing on the worn carpet answered Mr Wentworth quite normally. He heard his own voice, with just the right amount of amazement and innocence, saying, "Who, me? I'm not a witch, sir."

"I didn't say you were, Charles," Mr Wentworth replied. "I just said someone said you were. From the account I was given, you had a public row with Nan Pilgrim, in the course of which you spoke of worms and dead mice, and a number of other unpleasant things."

The part of Charles left standing on the carpet

answered indignantly, "Well I did. But I was only saying some of the things *she* said at lunch. You were there, sir. Didn't you hear her, sir?" Meanwhile, the part of Charles hovering near the ceiling was thanking whatever lucky stars looked after witches that Mr Wentworth had chanced to sit opposite Nan Pilgrim at high table.

"I did," said Mr Wentworth. "I recognized your reference at once. But my informant thought you were reciting a spell."

"But I wasn't, sir," protested the part of Charles on the carpet.

"But you sounded as if you were," Mr Wentworth said. "You can't be too careful, Charles, in these troubled times. It sounds as if I'd better explain the position to you."

He picked up his pipe to help him in the explanation. In the way of pipes, it had gone out by then. Mr Wentworth struck matches and puffed, and struck more matches and puffed. Smoke does not seem to mean fire where pipes are concerned. Mr Wentworth used ten matches before the pipe was alight. As Charles watched, it dawned on him that Mr Wentworth did not think he was a witch. Nor did Mr Wentworth seem to have noticed the odd way he had split into two. Perhaps the part of him hovering hear the ceiling was imaginary, and simply due to panic. As Charles thought this, he found the part of him near the ceiling slowly descending into the part of him standing normally on the carpet. By the time Mr Wentworth risked putting his pipe out again by pressing the matchbox down on it, Charles found himself in one piece. He was still fizzing all over with terror, it is true, but he was feeling nothing like so peculiar.

"Now, Charles," said Mr Wentworth. "You know witchcraft has always been illegal. But I think it's true to say that the laws against it have never been as strict as they are now. You've heard of the Witches' Uprising of course, in 1789, under the Archwitch Dulcinea Wilkes?"

Charles nodded. Everyone knew about Dulcinea. It was like being asked if you knew about Guy Fawkes.

"Now that," said Mr Wentworth, "was a respectable sort of uprising in its way. The witches were protesting against being persecuted and burnt. Dulcinea said, reasonably enough, that they couldn't help being born the way they were, and they didn't want to be killed for something they couldn't help. She kept promising that witches would use their powers only for good, if people would stop burning them. Dulcinea wasn't at all the awful creature everyone says, you know. She was young and pretty and clever – but she had a terribly hot temper. When people wouldn't agree not to burn witches, she lost her temper and worked a number of huge and violent spells. That was a mistake. It made people absolutely terrified of witchcraft, and when the uprising was put down, there were an awful lot of bone-fires and some really strict laws. But you'll know all that."

Charles nodded again. Apart from the fact that he had been taught that Dulcinea was an evil old hag, and a stupid one, this was what everyone knew.

"But," said Mr Wentworth, pointing his pipe at Charles, "what you may not know is that there was another, much more unpleasant uprising, just before you were born. Surprised? Yes, I thought you were. It was hushed up rather. The witches leading it were all unpleasant people, and their aim was to take over the country. The main conspirators were all civil servants and army generals, and the leader was a cabinet minister. You can imagine how scared and shocked everyone was at that."

"Yes, sir," said Charles. He had almost stopped being frightened by now. He found himself trying to imagine the Prime Minister as a witch. It was an interesting idea.

Mr Wentworth put his pipe in his mouth and puffed out smoke expressively. "The minister was burnt in

55

Trafalgar Square," he said. "And Parliament passed the Witchcraft Emergency Act in an effort to stamp out witches for good. That act, Charles, is still in force today. It gives the Inquisitors enormous powers. They can arrest someone on the mere suspicion of witchcraft — even if they're only your age, Charles."

"My age?" Charles said hoarsely.

"Yes. Witches keep on being born," said Mr Wentworth. "And it was discovered that the minister's family had known he was a witch since he was eleven years old. A lot of research has been done since on witches. There are a hundred different kinds of witch-detector. But most of the research has been towards discovering when witches first come into their powers, and it seems that most witches start at around your age, Charles. So, these days, the Inquisitors keep a special eye on all schools. And a school like this one, where at least half the pupils are witch-orphans anyway, is going to attract their notice at once. Understand?"

"No, sir," said Charles. "Why are you telling me?"

"Someone thought you recited a spell," Mr Wentworth said. "Think, boy! If I hadn't happened to know what you were really saying, you'd be under arrest by now. So now you'll have to be extra specially careful. Now do you see?"

"Yes, sir," said Charles. He was almost frightened again.

"Then off you go, back to devvy," said Mr Wentworth. Charles turned round and trudged over the threadbare carpet to the door. "And Charles," called Mr Wentworth. Charles turned round. "Take a black mark to remind you to be careful," said Mr Wentworth.

Charles opened the door. Two black marks in one evening! If you got three black marks in a week, you went to Miss Cadwallader and were in real trouble. Two black marks! Both for things which were not his fault! Charles turned round while he was closing the door and directed the full force of his nastiest double-barrelled glare at Mr Wentworth. He was seething.

He trudged up the corridor to the swing door, still seething. The swing door swung as he reached it, and, to his surprise, Miss Hodge came through it. Miss Hodge did not live in school. As Estelle had speedily found out and told everyone, she lived with her old father in town. She was not usually here in the evenings at all.

"Charles!" said Miss Hodge. "How convenient! Have you been seeing Mr Wentworth?"

It did not occur to Charles to wonder how Miss Hodge knew that. In his experience, teachers always knew far too much anyway. "Yes," he said.

"Then you can tell me which his room is," said Miss Hodge.

Charles pointed out the room and applied his shoulder to the swing door. He had just forced his way out into the corridor beyond, when it swung again and again let Miss Hodge through.

"Charles, are you sure Mr Wentworth was there? He didn't answer when I knocked."

"He was sitting by his fire," Charles said.

"Then perhaps I knocked at the wrong door," Miss Hodge said. "Can you come and show me? Would you mind very much?"

Yes I would mind, Charles thought. He sighed and went back through the swing door with Miss Hodge. Miss Hodge seemed pleased to have his company, which surprised him a little.

Miss Hodge was thinking how fortunate it was she had met Charles. Since the afternoon, she had been thinking carefully. And she saw that her next and most certain move towards marrying Mr Wentworth was to go to him and impulsively take back her accusation against Charles. It was unpleasant to think of anyone being burned, even if Charles did have the most evil glare of any boy she knew. She would look so generous. And here she was, actually with Charles, to prove she bore him no malice.

Charles looked at Mr Wentworth's name on the door and wondered how Miss Hodge could have got the wrong room.

"Oh," said Miss Hodge. "It was the right door. That's his name."

She knocked, and knocked again, with golden visions of her romance with Mr Wentworth growing as, together, they tried to protect Charles from the clutches of the Inquisitors. But there was no answer from the room. She turned to Charles in perplexity.

"Maybe he's gone to sleep," Charles said. "It was warm in there."

"Suppose we open the door and take a peep?" Miss Hodge said, fluttering a little.

"You do it," said Charles.

"No, you," said Miss Hodge. "I'll take all responsibility."

Charles sighed, and opened Mr Wentworth's door for the second time that evening. A gust of cold, smoky air blew in their faces. The room was dark, except for a faint glow from the cooling gas-fire. Even that vanished when Miss Hodge imperiously switched on the light and stood fanning the smoke away from her.

"Dear, dear," she said, looking round. "That man needs a woman's hand here. Are you sure he was here, Charles?"

"Just this minute," Charles said doggedly, but horror was beginning to descend on him. It was almost as if Mr Wentworth had never been. He walked over to the bald patch of carpet in front of the fire and felt the fire. It was quite hot. Mr Wentworth's pipe was lying in the pottery ashtray still, and that was warm too, but cooling in the icy air from the open window. Perhaps, Charles thought hopefully, Mr Wentworth had just felt tired and gone to bed. There was a door in the opposite wall, beyond the blowing curtains of the window, which was probably the door to his bedroom.

But Miss Hodge boldly walked over and opened that door. It was a cupboard, stuffed with schoolbooks. "He didn't go this way," she said. "Has he a bedroom along the corridor, do you know?"

"He must have," said Charles. But he knew Mr Wentworth had not gone down the corridor. He could not have come out of this room without Charles seeing him as he went to the swing door, or Miss Hodge seeing him as she pushed past Charles the other way. There was only one other possibility. Charles had looked daggers at Mr Wentworth. He had given him his very nastiest glare. And that glare had caused Mr Wentworth to disappear, just as Dan's running shoes had disappeared. It was what they called the Evil Eye.

"I don't think there's any point in waiting," Miss Hodge said discontentedly. "Oh well. I can speak to him tomorrow."

Charles was only too glad to go. He was only too glad to accompany Miss Hodge down to the door where she had left her bicycle. He talked to her most politely all the way. It kept his mind off what he had done. And he thought that if he talked hard enough and made himself truly charming, Miss Hodge might not realize that Charles had been the last person to set eyes on Mr Wentworth.

They talked of poems, football, bicycles, the caretaker's dog and Mr Hodge's garden. The result was that Miss Hodge mounted her bicycle and rode off, thinking that Charles Morgan was a very nice child once you got to know him. It made it all the better that she intended to withdraw her accusation against him. A teacher, she told herself, should always try to get to know her pupils.

Charles puffed out a big sigh of relief and trudged off again, weighted with new guilt. By the time he reached the classroom, nearly all the others had finished their work and were trooping off to choir practice. Charles had the room to himself, apart from Nan Pilgrim, who also seemed to be behindhand. They did not speak to one another, of course, but it was doubtful that either did much work. Nan was thinking miserably that if only she *was* a witch like Dulcinea Wilkes, she would not mind what anyone said. Charles was thinking about Mr Wentworth.

First the birds in Music, now Mr Wentworth. Being invisible to the senior didn't count, because no one knew about that. What terrified Charles was that he would seem to keep using witchcraft by accident, where it showed. If only he could stop himself doing that, then he still might have a chance. Miss Hodge might give him an alibi over Mr Wentworth, if he went on being nice to her. But how did you stop yourself working magic?

"This has been an awful day," Nan said, as she packed up to leave. "I'm so glad it's nearly over."

Charles stared at her, wondering how she knew. Then he packed up and left too. He was very much afraid that today was not over for him yet, by a long way. He had heard the Inquisitors usually came for you in the night. So they would come for him, as soon as someone discovered Mr Wentworth was missing. Charles thought about Mr Wentworth all the time he was washing. He had rather liked Mr Wentworth on the whole. He felt very bad about him. Perhaps the way to stop himself doing it again, to Mr Crossley or someone, was to think hard about how it felt to be burnt. It would hurt.

It hurts to be burnt, he repeated to himself as he undressed. *It hurts to be burnt.* He was shivering as he climbed into bed, and not only from the cold air in the long spartan dormitory.

Brian Wentworth was being beaten up again a few beds along from him. Brian was crouching on his bed with his arms over his head, while Simon Silverson and his friends hit him with their pillows. They were

60

laughing, but they meant it too. "Show off!" they were saying. "Boot-licker! Show off!"

Up till then, Charles had always been almost glad he was in this dormitory, and not in the next-door one like Nirupam, where Dan Smith ruled with his friends from 2X and 2Z. Now he wondered whether to sneak off and sleep in the lower school boys' playroom. Brian's yells – for Brian could never be hit quietly – kept cutting through Charles's miserable meditations and reminding him what he had done to Brian's father. It grew so bothersome that Charles nearly got out of bed and joined in hitting Brian too, just to relieve his feelings. But by this time he had gathered the reason for the pillows. Mr Brubeck had asked Brian to sing a solo at the school concert, and Brian had unwisely agreed. Everyone else knew that it was Simon's right to sing solo.

This meant that hitting Brian would be sucking up to Simon. That Charles would not do. He went back to his desperate wonderings. There was no way of keeping Mr Wentworth's disappearance secret that he could see. But there was quite a chance that no one would realize Charles had done it. So, if only he could think of some surefire way of stopping himself working magic by accident – that was it! Sure fire. It hurts to be burnt.

Charles got out of bed. He unhooked his glasses from his bed-rail, hooked them on his ears and thumped across to the flurry of pillows.

"Can I borrow the emergency candle for five minutes?" he said loudly to Simon.

Simon of course was dormitory monitor. He paused in belabouring Brian and became official. "The candle's only for emergencies. What do you want it for?"

"You'll see if you give it me," said Charles.

Simon hesitated, torn between curiosity and his usual desire never to give anyone anything. "You'll have to tell me what you want it for first. I can't let you have it for no reason."

61

"I'm not going to tell you," said Charles. "Just give it me."

Simon considered. Long experience of Charles Morgan had shown him that when Charles said he was not going to tell, nothing would make him tell, not pillows or even wild horses. His curiosity, as Charles had hoped, was thoroughly aroused. "If I give it you," he said righteously, "I shall be breaking the rules. You owe me compensation for risking getting into trouble, you know."

This was only to be expected. "What do you want?" said Charles.

Simon smiled graciously, wondering how great Charles's need was. "Your pocket money every week for the rest of term," he said. "How about that?"

"Too much," said Charles.

Simon turned away and picked up his pillow again. "Take it or leave it," he said. "That's my final offer."

"I'll take it," said Charles, hating Simon.

Simon turned back to him in astonishment. He had expected Charles either to protest or give up asking. His friends stared at Charles, equally astonished. In fact, by this time, nobody was hitting Brian any more. Here was something really odd going on. Even Brian was staring at Charles. How could anyone want a candle that much? "Very well," Simon said. "I'll accept your offer, Charles. But remember you promised in front of witnesses. You'd better pay up."

"I'll pay up," said Charles. "Every week when Mr Crossley gives us our money. Now give me the candle."

Simon, with busy efficiency, fetched his keyring from his blazer and unlocked the cupboard on the wall where the First Aid kit and the candle were kept. If a miracle happened, Charles thought, and the Inquisitors did not come for him after all, he had put himself in a true mess now. No pocket money until Christmas. That meant he could not pay for new running shoes. He would have to write five hundred lines every day for Mr Towers. But he did not really believe he would be around to do that very long. Everyone said the Inquisitors found witches whatever they did.

Simon put the candle in his hands. It was unlit, in a white enamel candle-holder. Charles looked at it. He looked up to see Simon and all the other boys, even Brian, grinning.

"You forgot to ask for matches," Simon pointed out.

Charles looked at him. He glared. He did more than glare. It was the nastiest look he had ever given anyone. He hoped it would shrivel Simon on the spot.

All that happened was that Simon stepped backwards from him. Even so, he looked as superior as ever. "But I'll give you the matches free," he said. "It's all part of the service." He tossed a box of matches towards Charles.

Charles put the candlestick down on the floor. With everyone staring at him, he struck a match and lit the candle. He knelt down beside it. *It hurts to be burnt*, he thought. *It hurts to be burnt*. He put out his finger and held it in the small yellow flame.

"Why on earth are you doing that?" asked Ronald West.

Charles did not answer. For a second, he thought the flame was not going to burn him. It just felt warm and wet. Then, quite suddenly, it was hot and it hurt very much indeed. It hurt, as Charles had expected, in quite a different way from cutting yourself or stubbing your toe. This was a much nastier pain, sharp and dull together, which brought Charles's back out in goose-pimples and jangled the nerves all the way up his arm. Imagine this all over you, he thought. *It hurts to be burnt*. He took hold of his wrist with his other hand and held it hard to stop himself snatching his finger out of the pain. *It hurts to be burnt*. It did hurt too. It was making sweat prickle out just beneath his eyes.

63

"It must be for a dare or a bet," he heard Simon saying. "Which is it? Tell, or I'll put the candle away again."

"A bet," Charles answered at random. *It hurts to be burnt. It hurts to be burnt.* He thought this over and over, intent on branding it into his brain – or into whatever part of him it was that did magic. *It hurts to be* – Oh, it hurts! – *hurts to be burnt.*

"Some people," Simon remarked, "make awfully stupid bets."

Charles ignored him and tried to keep his jerking finger steady. It was trying to jump out of the flame of its own accord. The finger was now red, with a white band across the red. He could hear a funny noise, a sort of tiny frizzling, as if his skin was frying. Then, suddenly, he could bear no more. He found himself snatching his finger away and blowing out the candle. The boys watching him all let out a sigh, as if they had been holding their breath.

"I suppose," Simon said discontentedly, as Charles handed him the candle back, "you make more money on this bet than you owe me now."

"No I don't," Charles said quickly. He was afraid Simon would be after that money too. Simon was quite capable of telling Mr Crossley about the candle if Charles did not pay. "I don't get anything. The bet was to burn my finger right off."

The prefect on duty appeared in the doorway, shouting, "Lights out! No more talking!"

Charles got into bed, sucking his burnt finger, hoping and praying that he had now taught himself not to work magic by accident. His tongue could feel a big pulpy blister rising between the first and second joint of his finger. It hurt more than ever.

Simon said, out of the darkness, "I always knew Charles Morgan was mad. What a brainless thing to do!"

Ronald West said, "You don't expect brains in an animal."

"Animals have more sense," said Geoffrey Baines.

"Charles Morgan," said Simon, "is a lower life form."

These kind of comments went on for some time. It was perfectly safe to talk because there was always such a noise from the next dormitory. Charles lay and waited for them to stop. He knew he was not going to sleep. Nor did he. Long after Simon and his friends had fallen silent, long after two prefects and the master in charge had come along and shut up the boys next door, Charles lay stiff as a log of wood, staring up into the shadows.

He was frightened – terrified. But the terror was now a dreary long-distance kind of terror, which he was sure he was going to feel all the time, for the rest of his life now. Suppose by some miracle, no Inquisitors came for him, then he was going to be afraid that they would, every minute of every day, for years and years. He wondered if you learnt to get used to it. He hoped so, because at this moment he felt like springing out of bed and confessing, just to get it over. What would Simon say, if Charles jumped up shouting "I'm a witch!" Probably he would think Charles was mad. It was funny that Simon had not disappeared too. Charles sucked his finger and puzzled over that. He certainly hated Simon enough. He had not hated Mr Wentworth at all really – or only in the way you hate any master who gives you a black mark you do not deserve. Perhaps witchcraft had to be sort of clinical to work properly.

Then Charles thought of his other troubles. Two black marks in one day. No running shoes. No money. Five hundred lines a day. And none of it was his fault! It was not his fault he had been born a witch, either, for that matter. It was all so unfair! He wished he did not have to feel so guilty about Mr Wentworth on top of it all. *It hurts to be burnt.*

Charles's thoughts slowly grew less connected after this point. He realized afterwards that he must have been to sleep. But if it was sleep, it was only a light horrified doze, in which his thoughts kept on clanking about in his head, as if he was a piece of machinery with the switch jammed to ON. But he did not know he had been to sleep. It seemed to him at the time that he sat up in bed after thinking things out in a perfectly orderly way. It was all quite obvious. He was a witch. He dared not be found out. Therefore he had to use some more witchcraft in order not to be found out. In other words, he had better go somewhere private like the toilets downstairs and conjure up first Mr Wentworth and then his running shoes.

Chapter Six

Charles got up. He remembered to put on his glasses. He even thought of arranging his bedclothes in heaps to make it look as if he was still in bed. He could see to do that by the dim light shining in from the corridor. By that light, he could see to creep past the sleeping humps of all the other boys. He crept out into the corridor, which seemed light as day by comparison.

There was a lot of noise coming from the next dormitory. There was rustling, and some heavy thumps, followed by some giggles hurriedly choked off. Charles stopped. It sounded as if they were having one of their midnight feasts in there. The thumps would be the floorboards coming up so that they could get at their hidden food. It was a bad time to wander about. If the master in charge heard the noise, Charles would be caught too.

But the corridor remained empty. After a while, Charles dared to go on. He went along the corridor and down the dark pit of the concrete stairs at the end. It was cold. The heating, which was never warm anyway, was turned down for the night. The chill striking up through Charles's bare feet and in through his pyjamas served to wake him up a little. He wondered if it was the pain in his finger which had woken him in the first place. It was throbbing steadily. Charles held it against the cold wall to soothe it and, while his feet felt their way from stair to cold stair, he tried to plan what he would do. Mr Wentworth was obviously the most important one to get back – if he could. But he did need those running-shoes too.

"I'll practise on the shoes," Charles muttered. "If I get those, I'll try for Mr Wentworth."

He stumbled off the end of the stairs and turned left towards the toilets. They were in a cross-passage down at the end. Charles was halfway to the corner, when the cross-passage became full of dull moving light. A half-lit figure loomed there, swinging a giant torch. The moving light caught the small white creature trundling at the figure's heels. The caretaker and his dog were on their way to inspect the toilets for vandals.

Charles turned and tiptoed the other way. The passage promptly filled with a shrill yap, like one very small clap of thunder. The dog had heard him. Charles ran. Behind him, he heard the caretaker shout, "Who's there?" and come clattering along the passage.

Charles ran. He ran past the end of the stairs, hoping the caretaker would think he had gone up them again, and went on, with his arms out in front of him, until he met the swing-door beyond. Gently, he pushed the door open a small way. Softly, he slid round it, holding the edge of the door so that it would not thump shut and give him away. Then he stood there hoping.

It was no good. The caretaker was not fooled. A muzz of light grew in the glass of the door. The shadow of the stair-rails swung across it and fell away, and the light went on growing brighter as the caretaker advanced.

Charles let the door go and ran again, thumping along dark corridors until he had no idea where he was and could hardly breathe. He shook off the caretaker, but he lost himself. Then he ran round a corner and blinked in the orange light from a far-off street-light shining through a window. Beyond the window was the unmistakable door of the lower school boys' playroom. Even in that dim light, Charles knew the kick marks at the bottom of the door, and the cracked glass in the upper panel where Nirupam Singh had tried to hit Dan Smith and missed. It seemed like home just then. There were worse places to practise magic in, Charles thought. He opened the door and crept in.

In the faint light, someone else jumped round to face him.

Charles jumped back against the door. He squeaked. The other person squeaked. "Who are you?" they both said at once. Then Charles found the light switch. He moved it down and then back up in one swift waggle, dazzling both of them. What he saw made him lean against the door, confounded, blinking green darkness. The other person was Brian Wentworth. That was odd enough. But the oddest thing, in that dazzling moment of light, was that Charles had clearly seen that Brian was in tears. Charles was amazed. Brian, as was well known, never cried. He shrieked and yowled and yelled for mercy when he was hit, but he had never, ever been known to shed tears. Charles went very quickly from amazement to horror. For it clearly took something out of the ordinary to make Brian cry – and that thing must be that Brian had discovered his father was mysteriously missing.

"I came down to make it all right again," Charles said guiltily.

"What can *you* do?" said Brian's voice out of the dark, thick and throaty with crying. "The only reason you're better off than me is because you glare at people and they leave you alone. I wish I had a dirty look like yours. Then I could stop them getting at me and hitting me all the time!"

He began crying again, loud jerky sobs. Charles could hear the crying moving off into the middle of the playroom, but he could not see Brian at first for green dazzle. He really could not believe Brian minded being hit that much. It happened so often that Brian must be thoroughly used to it. By this time, he could see that

Brian was crouching in the centre of the concrete floor. Charles went over and crouched down facing him.

"Is that the only thing that's the matter?" he enquired cautiously.

"*Only!*" said Brian. "*Only thing!* What else do you want them to do? Tear me apart limb from limb or something! Sometimes I wish they would. I'd be dead then. I wouldn't have to put up with them getting at me then, hour after hour, day after day! I hate this school!"

"Yes," Charles said feelingly. "So do I." It gave him wonderful pleasure to say it, but it did not help bring the subject round to the disappearance of Mr Wentworth. He took a deep breath to encourage himself. "Er – have you seen your father —?"

Brian broke in, almost with a scream. "Of *course* I've been to my magicking father! I go to him nearly every day and ask him to let me leave this place. I went to him this afternoon and asked him. I said why couldn't I go to Forest Road School, like Stephen Towers does, and you know what he said? He said Forest Road was a private school and he couldn't afford it. Couldn't afford it!" Brian said bitterly. "I ask you! *Why* can't he afford it, if Mr Towers can? He must get paid twice as much as Mr Towers! I bet he earns almost as much as Miss Cadwallader. And he says he can't afford it!"

Charles wondered. He remembered the threadbare hearthrug and the holes in Mr Wentworth's slippers. That looked like poverty to him. But he supposed it could be meanness. And that brought him back to his guilt. With Mr Wentworth gone, Brian would have to stay at Larwood House for ever. "But have you seen your father since then?" he asked.

"No," said Brian. "He told me not to keep coming whining to him." And he began to cry again.

So Brian had not found out yet. Charles felt huge relief. There was still time to get Mr Wentworth back. But that meant that it really was only being got at which was making Brian so unhappy. Despite the evidence, that surprised Charles. Brian always seemed so perky and unconcerned.

Brian was talking again, through his sobs. "Whatever I do," he said, "they get at me. I can't help my father being a teacher here! I can't help being good at things! I didn't *ask* Mr Brubeck to give me a solo to sing. He just did. But of course magicking Simon Silverson thinks *he* ought to sing it. That's the thing I hate most," Brian said vehemently. "The way everyone does what Simon Silverson says!"

"I hate him too," said Charles. "Badly."

"Oh it doesn't matter how *we* feel," Brian said. "Simon's word is law. It's like that game – you know, *Simon Says* – where you have to do things if they say *Simon Says* first. And what is he anyway? A stuck up —"

"Prat," said Charles, "who sucks up to teachers —"

"With golden hair and a saintly expression. Don't forget the smug look," said Brian.

"Who could?" said Charles. "He kicks you in the pants, and then looks as if it's your fault his foot came up."

He was enjoying this. But he stopped enjoying it when Brian said, "Thanks for stopping them hitting me this evening. What gave you the idea of burning your finger like that? And trust Simon Silverson to rip you off all your money just for a candle!" Brian hesitated a second and then added, "I suppose I'd better pay you half of it."

Charles just managed to stop himself backing away. That would be really unkind. But what was he to do now? Brian clearly thought Charles had come downstairs in order to comfort him. Probably he would expect Charles to be his friend in future. Well, Charles supposed, he had deserved it. This was what you got for putting the Evil Eye on people's fathers. But quite apart from Mr Wentworth, quite apart from the fact that Brian was lowest of the low in 2Y, even quite apart from

71

the fact that Charles did not like Brian, Charles knew he could not be friends with anyone now. He was a witch. He could get anyone who was friends with him arrested too.

"You mustn't pay me anything," he said. "You don't owe me a thing."

Brian seemed distinctly relieved. "Then I'll tell you something instead," he said. "I've had enough of this place. If my father won't take me away, I'm going to *run* away."

"Where to?" said Charles. He had thought about running away himself, a while back, but he had had to give up the idea because there was nowhere to run away to.

"No idea," said Brian. "I shall just go."

"Don't be a fool," said Charles. This was one friendly thing he could say at least. "You have to plan it properly. If you just go, they'll call in tracker dogs and bring you straight back. Then you'll be punished."

"But I'll go mad if I stay here!" Brian said hysterically. Then he appeared to stop and consider, with his teeth chattering. "I think I see a way," he said.

By this time, both of them were shivering. It was cold in the playroom. Charles wondered how he could make Brian go back to bed without going himself. He could not think of a way. So they both went on crouching face to face in the middle of the concrete floor, until there was a sudden little pattering outside the cracked door. Both of them jumped.

"Caretaker's dog," whispered Charles.

Brian giggled. "Stupid creature. It looks just like Theresa Mullett's knitting."

Charles, before he could stop himself, gave a shriek of laughter. "It does! It does!"

"Shut up!" hissed Brian. "The caretaker's coming!"

Sure enough, the cracked glass of the door was showing misty torchlight. The dog began yapping furiously on the other side of it. It knew they were there.

Brian and Charles sprang up and fled, through the playroom and out of its other door. As it thumped shut behind them, the cracked door thumped open and the hollow playroom echoed with the dog's little thunder-claps. Without a word, Charles ran one way and Brian ran another. Where Brian went, Charles never knew. He heard the second door thump open as he ran, and the patter of tiny feet behind him. Charles held his glasses on and ran desperately. It was just like the seniors in the shrubbery. What made everyone chase *him*? Did he smell of witch, or something?

He found an outside door, but it was locked. He pelted on. Behind him, in the distance, he could hear the caretaker bawling to his dog to come back. That made the dog hesitate. Charles, quite terrified by now, put on a spurt and hurled himself through the next door he came to.

There was a feeling of large cold space inside this door. Charles went forward a few cautious steps and hit his foot with a clang on a row of steel chairs. He stood frozen, waiting to be discovered. He could hardly hear for the blood banging in his ears at first. Then he found he could hear the dog yapping again, somewhere quite far off. It seemed to have lost him. At the same time, he found he could see the faint shapes of huge windows, high up, beyond the chairs. He was in the school hall.

It came to Charles that he was not going to get a better opportunity than this. Better summon up his shoes at once. No – forget the shoes. Mr Wentworth was far more urgent. Get Mr Wentworth, and when Mr Wentworth appeared, perhaps Charles could put in a word about Brian.

It was at this point that Charles realized that he dared not fetch Mr Wentworth back. If Mr Wentworth did not know who had made him vanish, he *would* know as soon as he arrived back and found Charles.

"Flaming witches!" Charles moaned. "Why didn't I think?"

The dog, not too distant, gave another yap. Hunted and undecided, Charles shuffled forwards and fell across more chairs. He was in a perfect maze of chairs. He stood where he was and tried to think.

He could still get the shoes, he thought. He could say he was sleepwalking with worry about them when the caretaker found him. Uncertainly, he held up both arms. That dog was definitely coming nearer again.

"Shoes," Charles said hurriedly, and his voice cracked with fear and cold and lack of breath. "Shoes. Come to me. Hey presto. Abracadabra. Shoes, I say!" The dog sounded almost outside the hall door now. Charles made dragging movements with his hands and then crossed them over his chest. "Shoes!"

A thing that, by the sound, could have been a shoe, fell on the chair next to him. Despite the yapping dog, Charles grinned with pleasure. The second shoe fell on the other side of him. Charles put out groping hands to find them. And two more fell on his head. Several more flopped down near his feet. Now he could hear shoes dropping down all round him. He seemed to be in the centre of a rain of shoes. And the dog was scrabbling at the door now as it yapped. A wellington boot, by the feel, hit Charles on the shoulder as he turned and groped along the chairs, stumbling over gym shoes, football boots and lace-ups, with more and more dropping round him as he groped.

The caretaker was nearly at the door now. Charles could see the torchlight advancing through the glass. It helped him find his way. For he knew there was no question of any nonsense about sleepwalking now. He had to get out, and fast. He floundered among the pattering, flopping shoes, between the rows of chairs to the side of the hall, where he bolted for the door that the teachers came in by. Pitch dark descended on the other side of that door. Charles supposed he was in the staff room, but he never knew for sure. Stumbling, with his hands held out in front of him, dreamlike with panic, he fell over a stool. As he picked himself up, he remembered his second witch, the one who came through the garden. He should have thought about her earlier, he realized, as he knocked into a pile of books. She had said you couldn't work magic when you were frightened. She was right. Something had gone very wrong out there in the hall. Obviously, Charles thought, having a mad tangle with a coat of some kind, you needed to be cool and collected to be sure of getting it right. Oh thank Heaven! Here was a door.

Charles plunged out of the door and found himself not far from the main stairs. He fled up them. As he went, his thumb found the fat painful blister on his finger and he rubbed it as he ran upwards. What a waste! What an utter waste of money! Burning his finger seemed to have taught him nothing at all. And here was the beautiful, welcoming green night-light of the dormitory corridors. Not far now.

Charles did not remember getting into bed. His last clear thought was to wonder whether Brian had come back or whether he had run away on the spot. When the clanging bell dragged him awake in the morning, he had a sort of feeling that he had gone to sleep on the dormitory floor near the end of Brian's bed. But no. He was in his own bed. His glasses were hooked on the bed-rail. He began to hope he had dreamed last night. But, long before he was awake enough to sit up and yawn, the room filled with indignant voices.

"I can't find my shoes!"

"I say, what's happened to all our shoes?"

"My slippers aren't here either!"

As Charles managed to sit up, Simon said, "Are you a shoe-thief now, Brian?" and smacked Brian's head in a jolly, careless way, to show he did not think Brian was capable of being anything so enterprising. Brian was kneeling up in bed, looking as sleepy as Charles felt. He did not answer Simon or look at Charles.

In the next dormitory, they had no shoes either. And a senior could be heard coming down the corridor, shouting, "Hey! Have you lot pinched our shoes?"

Everyone was annoyed. Everyone thought there was a practical joke going on. Charles just hoped they would go on thinking that. Everyone was forced to go without shoes and slither around in socks. Charles's shoes were missing too – he was glad he seemed to have been that thorough – and he was just dragging on a second pair of socks, when rumour spread along the corridor. In the way of rumours, it was quite mysterious. Nobody knew who started it.

"We're to go down to the hall. All the shoes are there."

Charles joined the slithering rush for the hall. That rush was joined in the downstairs passage by all the girls, also in socks, also making for the hall. The seniors naturally occupied the door of the hall. Everyone from the lower school streamed outside into the quadrangle to look through the hall windows. There, everyone's first reaction was simple awe.

A school with six hundred pupils owns an awful lot of shoes. There would be twelve hundred even if everyone simply had one pair. But at Larwood House, everyone had to have special shoes for almost everything they did. So you had to add to that number all the gym shoes, running shoes, tennis shoes, trainers, dancing shoes, spare shoes, best shoes, sandals, football boots, hockey boots, wellington boots and galoshes. The number of shoes is swiftly in thousands. Add to those all the shoes owned by the staff too: Miss Cadwallader's characteristic footgear with heels like cotton reels; the cook's extra-wide fitting; the groundsman's hobnails; Mr

Crossley's hand-made suede; Mr Brubeck's brogues; Matron's sixteen pairs of stiletto heels; someone's purple fur boots; and even the odd pair of riding boots; not to speak of many more. And you have truly formidable numbers. The chairs in the hall were buried under a monstrous mountain of shoes.

Amid the general marvelling, Theresa's voice was heard. "If this is someone's idea of a joke, I don't think it's funny. My bedsocks are all muddy!" She was wearing blue fluffy bedsocks over her school socks.

After this, there was something of a free-for-all. People scrambled in through doors and windows and slithered on the pile of shoes, digging for shoes they thought were theirs – or, failing that, simply a pair that would fit.

Until a voice began bellowing, "OUT! GET OUT ALL OF YOU! LEAVE ALL THE SHOES THERE!"

Charles was pushed backwards by the rather slower rush to leave the hall, and had to crane to see who was shouting. It was Mr Wentworth. Charles was so amazed that he stopped moving and was left by a sort of eddy inside the hall, just by the door. From there, he could clearly see Mr Wentworth walking down the edge of the pile of shoes. He was wearing his usual shabby suit, but his feet were completely bare. Otherwise there was nothing wrong with him at all. After him came Mr Crossley in bright yellow socks and Mr Brubeck with a large hole in the heel of his left sock. After them came the caretaker. After him of course trundled the caretaker's dog, which was manifestly wishing to raise a leg against the pile of shoes.

"I don't know who done it!" the caretaker was protesting. "But I know there was people sneaking round my building half the night. The dog nearly caught one, right in this very hall."

"Did you come in here and investigate?" Mr Wentworth said.

"Door was shut," said the caretaker. "Thought it was locked."

Mr Wentworth turned from him in disgust. "Someone was pretty busy in here all last night," he said to Mr Crossley, "and he didn't even look!"

"Thought it was locked," repeated the caretaker.

"Oh shut up!" snapped Mr Wentworth. "And stop your dog peeing on that shoe. It's Miss Cadwallader's."

Charles slipped out into the corridor, trying to keep the grin on his face down to decent proportions. Mr Wentworth was all right. He must have slipped off to bed after all last night, while Miss Hodge was asking Charles the way. And, better still, everyone thought the shoes had arrived in the hall quite naturally. Charles could have danced and sung.

But here was Dan Smith beside him. That sobered Charles somewhat. "Hey," said Dan. "Did those seniors catch you last night?"

"No, I ran away," Charles replied airily.

"You must have run pretty fast!" said Dan. It was grudging, but it was praise, coming from Dan. "Know anything about who did these shoes?" Dan asked, jerking his head towards the hall.

Charles would dearly have loved to say it was him and watch the respect grow on Dan's face. But he was not that much of a fool. "No," he said.

"I do," said Dan. "It was the witch in our class, I bet."

Mr Wentworth appeared in the doorway of the hall. There were loud shushings up and down the packed corridor. "Breakfast is going to be late," Mr Wentworth shouted. He looked very harrowed. "You can't expect the kitchen staff to work without shoes. You are all to go to your classrooms and wait there. Meanwhile, teachers and sixth formers are going to be working hard laying all the shoes out in the main quadrangle. When you are called – *when* you are called, understand? – you are to come by classes and pick out the shoes which are yours. Off you all go. Sixth form stay behind."

Everyone milled off in a reluctant crowd. Charles was so pleased with himself that he risked grinning at Brian. But Brian was staring dreamily at the wall and did not notice. He did not move or even yell when Simon slapped him absent-mindedly round the head. 'Where's Nan Pilgrim?" Simon asked, laughing. "Turned herself invisible?"

Nan was keeping out of the way, lurking in the top corridor by the girls' bathrooms. From there, she had an excellent view of the quadrangle being covered with row upon row of shoes, and the kitchen ladies tiptoeing about the rows in stockings looking for their work-shoes. It did not amuse her. Theresa's friend Delia Martin and Estelle's friend Karen Grigg had already made it quite plain that they thought it was Nan's doing. The fact that these two normally did not speak to one another, or to Nan either, only seemed to make it worse.

Chapter Seven

Breakfast was ready before 2Y had been called to find their shoes. Theresa was forced to walk through the corridors in her blue bedsocks. They were, by this time, quite black underneath, which upset her considerably. Breakfast was so late that assembly was cancelled. Instead, Miss Cadwallader stood up in front of high table, with her face all stringy with displeasure and one foot noticeably damp, and made a short speech.

"A singularly silly trick has been played on the school," she said. "The people who played it no doubt think it very funny, but they must be able to see by now what a stupid and dishonourable thing they have done. I want them to be honourable now. I want them to come to me and confess. And I want anyone else who knows or suspects who did it to be equally honourable and come and tell me what they know. I shall be in my study all morning. That is all."

"What is honourable," Nirupam said loudly, as everyone stood up, "about going and telling tales?"

By saying that, he did Nan a service, whether he meant to or not. No one in 2Y wanted a name for telling tales. Nobody went to Miss Cadwallader. Instead, they all went out into the quadrangle, where a little freezing drizzle of rain was now falling, and walked up and down the spread-out rows of damp footgear, finding their shoes. Nan was forced to go too.

"Oh look! Here comes Archwitch Dulcinea," said Simon. "Why did you do it to your own shoes too,

Dulcinea? Thought it would look more innocent, did you?"

And Theresa said, "Really, Nan! My bedsocks are ruined! It isn't funny!"

"Do something really funny now, Nan," Karen Grigg suggested.

"Hurry up!" Mr Crossley shouted from the shelter of the porch. Everyone at once became very busy turning over shoes. The only one who did not was Brian. He simply wandered about, staring into space. In the end, Nirupam found his shoes for him and bundled them into Brian's lax arms.

"Are you all right?" Nirupam asked him.

"Who? Me? Oh yes," Brian said.

"Are you sure? One of your eyes is sort of set sideways," Nirupam said.

"Is it?" Brian asked vaguely, and wandered off.

Nirupam turned severely to Simon. "I think you hit him on the head once too often."

Simon laughed, a little uneasily. Nirupam was a head taller than he was. "Nonsense! There's nothing in his head to get hurt."

"Well, you watch it," said Nirupam, and might have said more, except that they were interrupted by an annoyed outcry from Dan Smith.

"I'll get someone for this!" Dan was shouting. He was very pale and cross after last night's midnight feast, and he looked quite savage. "I'll get them even if they're a magicking senior. Someone's gone off with my running shoes! I can't find them anywhere."

"Look again, carefully!" Mr Crossley bawled from the porch.

This was a queer fact. Dan searched up and down the rows, and so did Charles, until their socks were soaked and their hair was trickling rain, but neither Dan's spikes nor Charles's were there. By this time, 1X, 1Z and 1Y had been allowed out to collect their shoes too before they all got too wet, and almost the only footgear left was the three odd football boots, the riding boots, and a pair of luminous green trainers that nobody seemed to want. Dan uttered such threats that Charles was glad that it did not seem to occur to Dan that this had anything to do with Charles Morgan.

But it meant that Charles had to go to Mr Towers next and confess that his running shoes had still not turned up. He was fed up as he stood and trickled rain outside the staff room. After all his trouble!

"I did look, sir," he assured Mr Towers.

Mr Towers glanced at Charles's soaking hair and rain-dewed glasses. "Anyone can stand in the rain," he said. "Are you paying for new ones or writing lines?"

"Doing lines," Charles said resentfully.

"In detention every evening until Christmas then," Mr Towers said. The idea seemed to please him. "Wait." He dodged back into the staff room and came out again with a fat old book. "Here," he said, handing the book to Charles. "Copy five hundred lines of this out every evening. It will show you what a real schoolboy should be like. When you've copied it all, I'll give you the sequel."

Charles stood in front of the staff room and looked at the book. It was called *The Pluckiest Boy in School*. It smelt of mildew. Inside, the pages were furry and brownish, and the first line of the story went: *"What ripping fun!" exclaimed Watts Minor. "I'm down for scrum half this afternoon!"*

Charles looked from this to the fat, transparent and useless blister on his finger and felt rather ill. "Magicking hell," he said.

"Good morning, Charles," said Miss Hodge, tripping towards the staff room, all fresh and unaware. "That looks a nice old book. I'm glad to see you doing some serious reading at last."

She was most disconcerted to receive one of Charles's

heaviest double-barrelled glares. What a moody boy he was to be sure! she thought as she neatly stripped off her raincoat. She was eqally surprised to find the staff room in some kind of uproar, with a pile of boots and shoes in the middle. Still, there was Mr Wentworth at last, flying past on his way somewhere else. Miss Hodge stood in his way.

"Oh, Mr Wentworth, I want to apologize for making that accusation against Charles Morgan." That was pretty generous of her, she thought, after the way Charles had just looked at her. She smiled generously at Mr Wentworth.

To her annoyance, Mr Wentworth simply said, "I'm glad to hear it," and brushed past her quite rudely. But he did have a lot on his mind, Miss Hodge realized, when Mr Crossley told her excitedly all about the shoes. She did not hold it against Mr Wentworth. She collected books – they had got spilled all over the floor somehow – and went off to give 2Y another English lesson.

She arrived to find Simon Silverson holding aloft *The Pluckiest Boy in School*. "Listen to this!" he was saying. *"Swelling with pride, Watts Minor gazed into the eyes of his one true friend. Here was a boy above all, straight alike in body and mind – "*

Theresa and Delia were screaming with laughter, with their faces buried in their knitting. Charles was glaring blue murder.

"Really, Simon!" said Miss Hodge. "That was unworthy of you." Simon looked at her in astonishment. He knew he never did anything unworthy. "But Charles," said Miss Hodge, "I do think you made rather an unfortunate choice of book." For the second time that day, Charles turned his glare on her. Miss Hodge flinched. Really, if she had not known now that Charles was a nice boy underneath, that glare of his would make her think seriously of the Evil Eye.

Nirupam held up his long arm. "Are we going to do

acting again?" he asked hopefully.

"No we are not," Miss Hodge said, with great firmness. "Get out your poetry books."

The lesson, and the rest of the morning, dragged past. Theresa finished her second bootee and cast on stitches for a matinee jacket. Estelle knitted quite a lot of a baby's bonnet. Brian gave up staring at the wall and instead seemed to be attacked by violent industry. Whenever anyone looked at him, he was scribbling furiously in a different exercise book.

Charles sat and brooded, rather surprised at the things going on in his mind. He was not frightened at all now. He seemed to be accepting the fact he was a witch quite calmly after all. No one had noticed. They all thought the witch was Nan Pilgrim, because of her name, which suited Charles very well. But the really strange thing was the way he had stopped being worried by the witch he had seen being burnt. He tried remembering him, cautiously at first, then boldly, when he found it did not bother him. Then he went on to the second witch, who came over the wall. Neither troubled him now. They were in the past: they were gone. It was like having toothache that suddenly stops. In the peace that came with this, Charles saw that his mind must have been trying to tell him he was going to grow up a witch. And now he knew, it stopped nagging him. Then, to see if this made him frightened, he thought of Inquisitors. *It hurts to be burnt*, he thought, and looked at his fat blister. It had taught him something after all. And that was: Don't get found out.

Good, thought Charles. And turned his mind to what he was going to do to Simon Silverson. Dan Smith next, but Simon definitely first. What could he do to Simon that would be worth nearly a whole term's pocket money? It was difficult. It had to be something bad enough, and yet with no connection with Charles. Charles was quite stumped at first. He wanted it to be

84

artistic. He wanted Simon to suffer. He wanted everyone else to know about it, but not to know it was Charles who did it. What *could* he do?

The last lesson beforc lunch was the daily PE. Today, it was the boys' turn in the gym. They were to climb ropes too. Charles sat by the wallbars and pretended to tie his gym-shoe. Unlike Nan, he could get up a rope if he wanted, but he did not want to. He wanted to sit and think what to do to Simon. Simon, of course, was one of the first to the ceiling. He saw Charles and shouted something down. The result was that someone from 2Z came and dug Charles in the back.

"Simon says you're to stop lazing about."

"Simon says that, does he?" said Charles. He stood up. He was inspired. It was something Brian had said last night. That game, *Simon Says*. Suppose it was not just a game. Suppose everything Simon said really came true. At the very worst it ought to be pretty funny. At best, people might even think Simon was a witch.

Charles went up a rope. He dragged himself up it, nice and slow and gentle, so that he could go on thinking. He was obviously not going to be able to stand anywhere near Simon to put the spell on him. Someone would notice. But instinct told Charles that this was not the kind of magic you could work at a distance. It was too strong and personal. What he needed, in order to do it safely, was something which was not Simon himself, but something which belonged to Simon so personally that any witchcraft worked on it would work on Simon at the same time – a detachable piece of Simon, really. What removable parts had Simon? Teeth, toenails, fingernails, hair? He could hardly go up to Simon and pull any of those off him. Wait a minute! Hair. Simon combed his hair this morning. With any luck, there might be some hair stuck in Simon's comb.

Charles slid jubilantly down the rope – so fast that he was reminded again that it hurts to be burnt. He had to blow on his hands to cool them. After lunch was the time. He could sneak up to the dormitory then.

After lunch proved to be important for Nan too. At lunch, she managed to escape Karen Grigg and Delia Martin by sitting at a table full of much older girls who did not seem to know Nan was there. They towered over her, talking of their own things. The food was almost as bad as yesterday, but Nan felt no urge to describe it. She rather wished she was dead. Then it occurred to her that if any of 2Y went and told a teacher she was a witch, she would be dead, quite soon after that. She realized at once that she did not wish she was dead. That made her feel better. No one had gone to a teacher yet, after all. "It's only their usual silliness," she told herself. "They'll forget about it by Christmas. I'll just have to keep out of their way till they do."

Accordingly, after lunch, Nan sneaked upstairs to lurk in the passage outside the girls' bathrooms again. But Karen Grigg had been keeping tabs on her. She and Theresa appeared in the passage in front of Nan. When Nan turned round to make off, she found Delia and the other girls coming along the passage from the other end.

"Let's go in this bathroom," Theresa suggested. "We want to ask you something, Nan."

Nan could tell there was an ordeal coming. For a moment, she wondered whether to charge Theresa and Karen like a bull and burst past them. But they would only catch her tonight in the dormitory. Best get it over. "OK," she said, and sauntered into the bathroom as if she did not care.

Almost at the same moment, Charles hastened furtively into the boys' dormitory. White and clean and cold, the beds stood like rows of deserted icebergs, each with its little white locker at its side. Charles hurried to Simon's. It was locked. Simon was an inveterate locker of things. Even his watch had a little key to lock it on his wrist. But Charles did not let that bother him. He held out his hand imperiously in front of the locked door. "Comb," he said. "Abracadabra."

Simon's comb came gliding out through the white wooden surface, like a fish swimming out of milk, and darted fishlike into Charles's hand. It was beautiful. Better still, there were three of Simon's curly golden hairs clinging to the teeth of the comb. Charles carefully pulled them off. He held the hairs in the finger and thumb of his left hand and carefully ran his right finger and thumb down the length of them. And down again. Over and over, he did it. "Simon Says," he whispered to them. "Simon Says, Simon Says. Whatever Simon says is true."

After about a minute, when he had done it often enough to give him the feeling that the spell was going to take, Charles carefully threaded the hairs back into the comb again. He did not intend to leave any evidence against himself. He had just finished, when Brian said, from behind him, "I want a bit of help from you, Charles."

Charles jumped as if Brian had shot him. He bent over, in white horror, to hide the comb in his hand and, with terrible guilty haste, gave it a push towards the locker. It went in, to his surprise, not quite like a fish this time – more like a comb being pushed through a door – but at least it went. "What do you want?" Charles said ungraciously to Brian.

"Take me down to Matron in the sick bay," Brian said.

It was a school rule that a person who felt ill had to find another person to take them to Matron. It had been made because, before that, the sick bay had been crowded with healthy people trying to get an afternoon off. The idea was that you could not deceive your friends. It did not work very well. Estelle Green, for instance, got Karen to take her to Matron at least twice a week. As far as Charles could see, Brian looked his usual pink and perky self, just like Estelle.

"You don't look ill to me," he said. He wanted to find Simon and see if the spell was working.

"How about this then?" said Brian. To Charles's surprise, he suddenly turned pale. He stared vaguely at the wall, with one eye pointing inwards slightly. "This is it," Brian said. "Don't I look rather as if I'd been hypnotized?"

"You look as if you've been hit on the head," Charles said rudely. "Get Nirupam to take you."

"He looked after me this morning," said Brian. "I want as many witnesses as possible. I helped you last night. You help me now."

"You didn't help me last night," said Charles.

"Yes I did," said Brian. "You came in and you went to sleep on the floor, just at the end of my bed. I got you in your bed. I even hooked your glasses on your bed-rail for you." And he looked at Charles, very meaningly.

Charles stared back. Brian was so thin and small that it was hard to believe he could lift anyone into bed. But, whether it was true or not, Charles realized that Brian had got him over a barrel. He knew Charles had been up last night. He had caught him with Simon's comb in his hands just now. Charles could not see why Brian wanted to go to Matron, but that was his own affair. "All right," he said. "I'll take you."

Inside the bathroom, on the other side of the quadrangle, the girls crowded in round Nan. "Where's Estelle?" asked Theresa.

"Outside, keeping watch," said Karen. "That's all she would do."

"What's this about?" Nan asked aggressively.

"We want you to do some proper witchcraft," said Theresa. "Here, where we can see you. We've none of us

88

seen any before. And we know you can. Come on. We won't give you away."

The other girls joined in. "Come on, Nan. We won't tell."

The bathroom was a very public one. There were six baths in it, in a row. As the girls all crowded forward, Nan backed away, down the space between two of the baths. This was evidently just what they had wanted. Delia said, "That's it." Heather said, "Fetch it out." And Karen bent and pulled the groundsman's old besom out from under the left-hand bath. Julia and Deborah seized it and propped it across the two baths in front of Nan, penning her in. Nan looked from it to them.

"We want you to get on it and fly about," Theresa explained.

"Everyone knows that's what witches do," said Karen.

"We're asking you very nicely," said Theresa.

Typical Theresa double-think, Nan thought angrily. She was not asking her nicely. It was a smiling jeer. But if anyone asked Theresa afterwards, she would say, with honest innocence, that she had been perfectly kind.

"We can prove you're a witch anyway, if you won't," Theresa said kindly.

"Yes, everyone knows that witches don't drown," said Delia. "You can put them right under water and they stay alive."

At this cue, Karen leaned over and put the plug in the nearest bath. Heather turned on the cold tap, just a little trickle, to show Nan they meant business.

"You know perfectly well," Nan said, "that I'm not a witch, and I can't fly on this broomstick. It's just an excuse to be nasty!"

"Nasty?" said Theresa. "Who's being nasty? We're asking you quite politely to ride the broomstick." Behind her, the tap trickled steadily into the bath.

89

"You can fetch all the shoes here again if you like," Delia said. "We don't mind which."

"But you've got to do *something*," said Karen. "Or how would you like a nice deep cold bath with all your clothes on?"

Nan was annoyed enough by that to put one leg over the broomstick in order to climb out and get at Karen. Seeing it, Theresa gave a delighted jump and a giggle. "Oh, she's going to ride!"

The rest of them joined in. "She's going to ride it! Ride it, Nan!"

Very red in the face, Nan stood astride the broom and explained, "I am not going to ride. I do not know how to ride. You know I can't. I know I can't. Look. Look at me. I am sitting on the broomstick." Unwisely, she sat. It was extremely uncomfortable and she was forced to bounce upright again. This amused everyone highly. Angrier than ever, Nan shouted, "How *can* I ride a broomstick? I can't even climb a rope!"

They knew that. They were falling about laughing, when Estelle burst in, screaming with excitement. "Come and look, come and look! *Look* at what Simon Silverson's doing!"

This caused a stampede to the door, to look out of the windows in the corridor. Nan heard cries of, "Good Heavens! Just look at that!" This was followed by a further stampede as everyone raced off down to the quadrangle.

Nan was left astride an old besom propped on two baths.

"Thank goodness!" was the first thing she said. She had been precious near crying. "Stupid hussies!" she said next. "As if I could ride this thing. Look at it!" She jogged the broom. "Just an old broom!" Then she noticed the water still trickling into the bath behind her. She leant sideways and back and turned off the tap.

That was the moment the old besom chose to rise

sharply to the ceiling.

Nan shrieked. She was suddenly dangling head-down over a bath of cold water. The broom staggered a bit under her weight, but it went on climbing, swinging Nan right over the water. Nan bent her leg as hard as she could over its knobby stick, and managed to clench one hand in its sparse brushwood end. The broom reached the ceiling and levelled out. It did not leave room for Nan to climb on top of it, even if she had possessed the muscles. Blood thudded in her head from hanging upside down, but she did not dare let go.

"Stop it!" she squealed at the broom. "Please!"

It took no notice. It simply went on a solemn, lopsided, bumping flight all round the bathroom, with Nan dangling desperately underneath it and getting this-way-and-that glimpses of hard white baths frighteningly far below.

"I'm glad this didn't happen while the others were here," she gasped. "I must look a right idiot!" She began to laugh. She must look so silly. "Do go down," she said to the broom. "Suppose someone else comes in here."

The broom seemed struck by this. It gave a little start and slanted steeply down towards the floor. As soon as the floor was near enough, Nan clutched the handle in both hands and tried to unhook her leg. A mistake. The broom went steeply up again and hovered where it was just too high for Nan to dare to fall off. But her arms were getting tired and she had to do something. Wriggling and squirming, she managed to kick herself over, until she was more or less lying along the knobby handle, looking down at the row of baths. She hooked her feet on the brush and stayed there, panting.

Now what was she to do? This broom seemed determined to be ridden. There was a sad feeling about it. Once, long ago, it had been ridden, and it missed its witch.

"But that's all very well," Nan said to it. "I really

91

daren't ride you now. Don't you understand? It's illegal. Suppose I promise to ride you tonight. Would you let me down then?"

There was a hesitating sort of hover to the broom.

"I swear to," said Nan. "Listen, I tell you what. You fly me down the passage to our dormitory. That will make a bit of a flight at least. Then you can hide yourself on top of the cupboard, right at the back. No one will see you there. And I'll promise to take you out tonight. What do you say?"

Though the broom could not speak, it evidently meant Yes! It turned and swept through the bathroom doorway in a glad swoop that made Nan seasick. It sped down the passage. She had to shut her eyes in order not to see the walls whirling by. It made a hair-raising turn into the dormitory. And it stopped there with such a jerk that Nan nearly fell round underneath it again.

"I see I shall have to train you," she gasped.

The broom gave an indignant buck and a bounce.

"I mean you'll have to train me," Nan said quickly. "Go down now. I have to get off you."

The broom hovered, questioning.

"I promised," Nan said.

At that, the broom came sweetly to the ground and Nan was able to get off, very wobbly in the legs. As soon as she was off, the broom fell to the floor, lifeless. "You poor thing!" Nan said. "I see. You need a rider to move at all. All right. Let's get you on top of the cupboard."

In this way, she missed the first manifestation of the *Simon Says* spell. Charles missed it too. Neither of them discovered how Simon first found out that everything he said came true. Charles left Brian with a thermometer in his mouth, staring cross-eyed at the wall, and trudged back to the quadrangle to find an excited group round Simon. At first, Charles thought that the brightness flaring at Simon's feet was simply the sun shining off a puddle. But it was not. It was a heap of gold coins.

People were passing him pennies and stones and dead leaves.

To each thing as he took it, Simon said, "This is a gold coin. This is another gold coin." When that got boring, he said, "This is a *rare* gold coin. These are pieces of eight. This is a doubloon..."

Charles shoved his way to the front of the crowd and watched, utterly disgusted. Trust Simon to turn things to his own advantage! Gold chinked down on the heap. Simon must have been a millionaire by this time.

With a great clatter of running feet, the girls arrived. Theresa, with her knitting-bag hanging on her arm, pushed her way to the front, beside Charles. She was so astonished at the size of the pile of gold that she crossed the invisible line and spoke to Simon.

"How are you *doing* it, Simon?"

Simon laughed. He was like a drunk person by this time. "I've got the Golden Touch!" he said. Of course this immediately became the truth. "Just like that king in the story. Look." He reached for Theresa's knitting. Theresa indignantly snatched the knitting away and gave Simon a push at the same time. The result was that Simon touched her hand.

The knitting fell on the ground. Theresa screamed, and stood holding her hand out, and then screamed again because her hand was too heavy to hold up. It dropped down against her skirt, a bright golden metal hand, on the end of an ordinary human arm.

Out of the shocked silence which followed, Nirupam said, "Be very careful what you say, Simon."

"Why?" said Simon.

"Because everything you say becomes true," Nirupam said.

Evidently, Simon had not quite seen the extent of his powers. "You mean," he said, "I haven't got the Golden Touch." Instantly, he hadn't. "Let's test this," he said. He bent down and picked up Theresa's knitting. It was

93

still knitting, in a slightly muddy bag.

"Put it down!" Theresa said faintly. "I shall go to Miss Cadwallader."

"No you won't," said Simon, and that was true too. He looked at the knitting and considered. "This knitting," he announced, "is really two little caretaker's dogs."

The bag began to writhe about in his hands. Simon hurriedly dropped it with a sharp chink, on to the heap of gold. The bag heaved. Little shrill yappings came from inside it, and furious scrabbling. One little white bootee-dog burst out of it, shortly followed by a second. They ran on little minute legs, down the heap of gold and in among people's legs. Everyone got rather quickly out of their way. Everyone turned and watched as the two tiny white dogs went running and running into the distance across the quadrangle.

Theresa started to cry. "That was my knitting, you beast!"

"So?" Simon said, laughing.

Theresa lifted up her golden hand with her ordinary one and hit him with it. It was stupid of her, because she risked breaking her arm, but it was certainly effective. It nearly knocked Simon out. He sat down heavily on his heap of gold. "Ow!" said Theresa. "And I hope that hurt!"

"It didn't," said Simon, and got up smiling and, of course, unhurt.

Theresa went for him again, double-handed.

Simon skipped aside. "You haven't got one golden hand," he said.

There was suddenly space where Theresa's heavy golden hand had been. Her arm ended in a round pink wrist. Theresa stared at it. "How shall I knit?" she said.

"I mean," Simon said carefully, "that you have two ordinary hands."

Theresa looked at her two perfectly ordinary human

94

hands and burst into strange, artificial-sounding laughter. "Somebody kill him for me!" she said. "Quickly!"

Nobody offered to. Everybody was too shattered. Delia took Theresa's arm and led her tenderly away. The bell rang for afternoon lessons as they went.

"This is marvellous fun!" Simon said. "From now on, I'm all in favour of witchcraft."

Charles trudged off to lessons, wondering how he could cancel the spell.

Chapter Eight

Simon arrived late for lessons. He had been making sure his heap of gold was safe. "I'm sorry, sir," he said to Mr Crossley. And sorry he was. Tears came into his eyes, he was so sorry.

"That's all right, Simon," Mr Crossley said kindly, and everyone else felt compelled to look at Simon with deep sympathy.

You can't win with people like Simon, Charles thought bitterly. Anyone else would have been in bad trouble by now. And it was exasperating the way nobody so much as dreamed of accusing Simon of witchcraft. They kept looking at Nan Pilgrim instead.

Nan felt much the same about Theresa. Theresa arrived ten minutes after Simon, very white and sniffing rather. She was led in tenderly by Delia, and received almost as much sympathy as Simon. "Just gave her an aspirin and sent her away!" Nan heard Delia whisper indignantly to Karen. "I do think she ought to have been allowed to lie down, after all she's been through!"

What about all *I've* been through? Nan thought. No, it was Theresa's right to be in the right, as much as it was Simon's.

Nan had been given the full story by Estelle. Estelle was always ready to talk in class, and she was particularly ready, now that Karen seemed to have joined Theresa's friends. She knitted away under her desk at her baby's bonnet, and whispered and whispered. Nor was she the only one. Mr Crossley kept calling for quiet, but the whispers and rustling hardly abated at all. Notes kept arriving on Nan's desk. The first to arrive was from Dan Smith.

Make me the same as Simon and I'll be your friend for ever it said.

Most of the other notes said the same. All were very respectful. But one note was different. This one said, *Meet me round the back after lessons. I think you need help and I can advise you.* It was not signed. Nan wondered about it. She had seen the writing before, but she did not know whose it was.

She supposed she did need help. She really was a witch now. No one but a witch could fly a broomstick. She knew she was in danger and she knew she should be terrified. But she was not. She felt happy and strong, with a happiness and strength that seemed to be welling up from deep inside her. She kept remembering the way she had started to laugh when the broomstick went flying round the bathroom with herself dangling underneath it, and the way she seemed to understand by instinct what the broom wanted. Hair-raising as it had been, she had enjoyed it thoroughly. It was like coming into her birthright.

"Of course, Simon always said you were a witch," Estelle whispered.

That reduced Nan's joy a little. There was another witch in 2Y, she did not doubt that. And that witch had, for some mad reason, made everything Simon said come true. He must be one of Simon's friends. And it was quite possible that Simon, while he was under the spell, had happened to say that Nan was a witch. So of course she would have become one.

Nan refused to believe it. She *was* a witch. She wanted to be one. She came of a long line of witches, stretching back beyond even Dulcinea Wilkes herself. She felt she had a *right* to be a witch.

All this while, Mr Crossley was trying to give 2Y a

Geography lesson. He had got to the point where he was precious near giving up and giving everyone detention instead. He had one last try. He could see that the unrest was centering on Simon, with a sub-centre round Nan, so he tried to make use of it by asking Simon questions.

"Now the geography of Finland is very much affected by the last Ice Age. Simon, what happens in an Ice Age?"

Simon dragged his mind away from dreams of gold and glory. "Everything is very cold," he said. A blast of cold air swept through the room, making everyone's teeth chatter. "And goes on getting colder, I suppose," Simon added unwisely. The air in the room swiftly became icy. 2Y's breath rolled out in steam. The windows misted over and froze, almost at once, into frosty patterns. Icicles began to grow under the radiators. Frost whitened the desks.

There was a chorus of shivers and groans, and Nirupam hissed, "*Watch* it!"

"I mean everything gets very hot," Simon said hastily.

Before Mr Crossley had time to wonder why he was shivering, the cold was replaced by tropical heat. The frost slid away down the windows. The icicles tinkled off the radiators. For an instant, the room seemed fine and warm, until the frozen water evaporated. This produced a thick, steamy fog. In the murk, people were gasping. Some faces turned red, others white, and sweat ran on foreheads, adding to the fog.

Mr Crossley put a hand to his forehead, thinking he might be starting flu. The room seemed so dim suddenly. "Some theories do say that an Ice Age starts with extreme heat," he said uncertainly.

"But I say everything is normal for this time of year," Simon said, desperately trying to adjust the temperature.

Instantly it was. The classroom reverted to its usual way of being not quite warm enough, though still a little damp. Mr Crossley found he felt better. "Stop talking nonsense, Simon!" he said angrily.

Simon, with incredulity, realized that he might get into trouble. He tried to pass the whole thing off in his usual lordly way. "Well, sir, nobody really knows a thing about Ice Ages, do they?"

"We'll see about that," Mr Crossley said grimly. And of course nobody did. When he came to ask Estelle to describe an Ice Age, Mr Crossley found himself wondering just why he was asking about something which did not exist. No wonder Estelle looked so blank. He rounded back on Simon. "Is this a joke of some kind? What are you thinking of?"

"Me? I'm not thinking of anything!" Simon said defensively. With disastrous results.

Ah! This is more like it! Charles thought, watching the look of complete vacancy growing on Simon's face.

Theresa saw Simon's eyes glaze and his jaw drop and jumped to her feet with a scream. "Stop him!" she screamed. "Kill him! Do something to him before he says another word!"

"Sit down, Theresa," said Mr Crossley.

Theresa stayed standing up. "You wouldn't believe what he's done already!" she shouted. "And now look at him. If he says a word in that state —"

Mr Crossley looked at Simon. The boy seemed to be pretending to be an idiot now. What was the matter with everyone? "Take that look off your face, Simon," he said. "You're not that much of a fool."

Simon was now in a state of perfect blankness. And in that state, people have a way of picking up and echoing anything that is said to them. "Not that much of a fool," he said slurrily. The vacancy of his face was joined by a look of deep cunning. Perhaps that was just as well, Charles thought. There was no doubt that Theresa had a point.

"Don't *speak* to him!" Theresa shouted. "Don't you understand? It's every word he says! And—" She swung round and pointed at Nan. "It's all *her* fault!"

Before lunch, Nan would have quailed in front of Theresa's pointing finger and everyone's eyes turned on her. But she had ridden a broomstick now, and things were different. She was able to look scornfully at Theresa. "What nonsense!" she said.

Mr Crossley was forced to agree that Nan was right. "Don't be ridiculous, Theresa," he said. "I told you to sit down." And he relieved his feelings by giving both Theresa and Simon an hour in detention.

"Detention!" Theresa exlaimed, and sat down with a bump. She was outraged.

Simon, however, uttered a cunning chuckle. "You think you've got me, don't you?" he said.

"Yes, I do," said Mr Crossley. "Make it an hour and a half."

Simon opened his mouth to say something else. But here Nirupam intervened. He leant over and whispered to Simon, "You're very clever. Clever people keep their mouths shut."

Simon nodded slowly, with immense, stupid wisdom. And, to Charles's disappointment, he seemed to take Nirupam's advice.

"Get your journals out," Mr Crossley said wearily. There should be some peace now at least, he thought.

People opened their journals. They spread today's page in front of them. They picked up pens. And, at that point, even those who had not realized already, saw that there was almost nothing they dared write down. It was most frustrating. Here they were, with real, interesting events going on for once, and plenty of things to say, and almost none of it was fit for Miss Cadwallader's eyes. People chewed pens, shifted, scratched their heads, and stared at the ceiling. The most pitiable ones were those who were planning to ask Nan to endow them with the Golden Touch, or instant fame, or some other good thing. If they described any of the magic Nan was thought to have done, she would be arrested for witchcraft, and they would have killed the goose that laid the golden eggs.

Nan Pilgrim is not really a witch, Dan Smith wrote, after much hard thinking. He had rather a stomach ache after last night's midnight feast and it made his mind go slow. *I never thought she was really, it was just Mr Crossley having a joke. There was a practical joke this morning, it must have been hard work pinching everyone's shoes like that and then someone pinched my spikes and got me really mad. The caretakers dog peed—* And there Dan stopped, remembering Miss Cadwallader would read this too. Got quite carried away there, he thought.

No comment again today, Nirupam wrote swiftly. *Someone is riding for a fall. Not that I blame them for this afternoon, but the shoes were silly.* He put down his pen and went to sleep. He had been up half the night eating buns from under the floorboards.

My bedsocks were ruined, Theresa complained in her angel-writing. *My knitting was destroyed. Today has been awful. I do not want to tell tales and I know Simon Silverson is not in his right mind but someone should do something. Teddy Crossley is useless and unfair and Estelle Green always thinks she knows best but she can't keep her knitting clean. Matron was unfair too. She sent me away with an aspirin and she let Brian Wentworth lie down and I was* really *ill. I shall never speak to Nan Pilgrim again.*

Most people, though they could not attain Theresa's eloquence, managed to write something in the end. But three people still sat staring at blank paper. These were Simon, Charles and Nan.

Simon was very cunning. He was clever. He was thoroughly suspicious of the whole thing. They were trying to catch him out somehow. The safest and cleverest thing was not to commit anything to writing. He was sure of that. On the other hand, it would not do to let everyone know how clever he had gone. It would look peculiar. He ought to write just one thing. So, after more than half an hour of deep thought, he wrote: *Doggies*. It took him five minutes. Then he sat back, confident that he had fooled everyone.

Charles was stumped because he simply had no code for most of the things which had happened. He knew he had to write something, but the more he tried to think, the more difficult it seemed. At one point, he almost went to sleep like Nirupam. He pulled himself together. Think! Well, he could not write *I got up* for a start, because he had almost enjoyed today. Nor could he write *I didn't get up* because that made no sense. But he had better mention the shoes, because everyone else would. And he could talk about Simon under the code of potatoes. Mr Towers could get a mention too.

It was nearly time for the bell before Charles sorted all this out. Hastily he scrawled: *Our shoes all went to play Games. I thought about potatoes having hair hanging on a rope. I have Games with a bad book.* As Mr Crossley told them to put away their journals, Charles thought of something else and dashed it down. *I shall never be hot again.*

Nan wrote nothing at all. She sat smiling at her empty page, feeling no need to describe anything. When the bell went, as a gesture, she wrote down the date: 30 October. Then she shut her journal.

The instant Mr Crossley left the room, Nan was surrounded. "You got my note?" people clamoured at her. "Can you make it that whenever I touch a penny it turns to gold? Just pennies."

"Can you make my hair go like Theresa's?"

"Can you give me three wishes every time I say Buttons?"

"I want big muscles like Dan Smith."

"Can you get us ice-cream for supper?"

"I need good luck for the rest of my life."

Nan looked over at where Simon sat, hunched up with cunning and darting shrewd, stupid looks at Nirupam, who was sitting watchfully over him. If it was Simon who was responsible, there was no knowing when he would say something to cancel her witchcraft. Nan refused to believe it *was* Simon, but it was silly to make rash promises, whatever had made her a witch.

"There isn't time to work magic now," she told the clamouring crowd. And when that brought a volley of appeals and groans, she shouted, "It takes *hours*, don't you understand? You don't only have to mutter spells and brew potions. You have got to go out and pick strange herbs, and say stranger incantations, at dawn and full moon, before you can even begin. And when you've done all that, it doesn't necessarily work straight away. Most of the time, you have to fly round and round the smoking herbs all night, chanting sounds of unutterable sweetness, before anything happens at all. Now do you see?" Utter silence greeted this piece of invention. Much encouraged, Nan added, "Besides, what have any of you done to deserve me going to all that trouble?"

"What indeed?" Mr Wentworth asked, from behind her. "What exactly is going on here?"

Nan spun round. Mr Wentworth was right in the middle of the room and had probably heard every word. Around her, everyone was slinking back to their seats. "That was my speech for the school concert, sir," she said. "Do you think it's any good?"

"It has possibilities," said Mr Wentworth. "But it will need a little more working up to be quite good enough. Maths books out, please."

Nan sank down into her seat, weak with relief. For one awful moment, she had thought Mr Wentworth might have her arrested.

"I said Maths books out, Simon," Mr Wentworth said. "Why are you giving me that awful cunning look? Is it such a peculiar thing to ask?"

Simon considered this. Nirupam, and a number of other people, doubled their legs under their chairs, ready to spring up and gag Simon if necessary. Theresa once more jumped to her feet.

"Mr Wentworth, if he says another word, I'm not staying!"

Unfortunately, this attracted Simon's attention. "You," he said to Theresa, "stink."

"He seems to have spoken," said Mr Wentworth. "Get out and stand in the corridor, Theresa, with a black mark for bad behaviour. Simon can have another, and the rest of us will have a lesson."

Theresa, redder in the face than anyone had ever seen her, raced for the door. She could not, however, beat the truly awful smell which rolled off her and filled the room as she ran.

"Pooh!" said Dan Smith.

Somebody kicked him, and everybody looked nervously at Mr Wentworth to see if he could smell it too. But, as often happens to people who smoke a pipe, Mr Wentworth had less than the average sense of smell. It was not for five minutes, during which he had written numerous things on the board and said many more, none of which 2Y were in a fit state to attend to, that he said, "Estelle, put down that grey bag you're knitting and open a window, will you? There's rather a smell in here. Has someone let off a stink-bomb?"

Nobody answered. Nirupam resourcefully passed Simon a note, saying, *Say there is no smell in here.*

Simon spelled it out. He considered it carefully, with his head on one side. He could see there was a trick in it somewhere. So he cunningly decided to say nothing.

Luckily, the open window, though it made the room almost as cold as Simon's Ice Age, did slowly disperse the smell. But nothing could disperse it from Theresa, who stood in the passage giving out scents of sludge, kippers and old dustbins until the end of afternoon school.

When the bell had rung and Mr Wentworth swept from the room, everyone relaxed with a groan. No one had known what Simon was going to say next. Even Charles had found it a strain. He had to admit that the results of his spell had taken him thoroughly by surprise.

Meanwhile, Delia and Karen, with most of Theresa's main friends, were determined to retrieve Theresa's honour. They surrounded Simon. "Take that smell off her at once," Delia said. "It's not funny. You've been on at her all afternoon, Simon Silverson!"

Simon considered them. Nirupam leapt up so quickly that he knocked over his desk, and tried to put his hand over Simon's mouth. But he got there too late. "You girls," said Simon, "all stink."

The result was almost overpowering. So was the noise the girls made. The only girls who escaped were the lucky few, like Nan, who had already left the room. It was clear something had to be done. Most people were either smelling or choking. And Simon was slowly opening his mouth to say something else.

Nirupam left off trying to pick up his desk and seized hold of Simon by his shoulders. "You can break this spell," he said to him. "You could have stopped it straight away if you had any brain at all. But you would be greedy."

Simon looked at Nirupam in slow, dawning annoyance. He was being accused of being stupid. Him! He opened his mouth to speak.

"Don't *say* anything!" everyone near him shouted.

Simon gazed round at them, wondering what trick they were up to now. Nirupam shook him. "Say this after me," he said. And, when Simon's dull, cunning eyes turned to him, Nirupam said, slowly and loudly, "Nothing I said this afternoon came true. Go on. Say it."

105

"*Say* it!" everyone yelled.

Simon's slow mind was not proof against all this yelling. It gave in. "Nothing I said this afternoon came true," he said obediently.

The smell instantly stopped. Presumably everything else was also undone, because Simon at once became his usual self again. He had almost no memory of the afternoon. But he could see Nirupam was taking unheard-of liberties. He looked at Nirupam's hands, one on each of his shoulders, in surprise and annoyance. "Get off!" he said. "Take your face away."

The spell was still working. Nirupam was forced to let go and stand back from Simon. But, as soon as he had, he plunged back again and once more took hold of Simon's shoulders. He stared into Simon's face like a great dark hypnotist. "Now say," he said, "Nothing I say is going to come true in the future."

Simon protested at this. He had great plans for the future. "Now, look here!" he said. And of course Nirupam did. He looked at Simon with such intensity that Simon blinked as he went on with his protest. "But I'll fail every exam I ever ta–a–a–ake – !" His voice faded out into a sort of hoot, as he realized what he had said. For Simon loved passing exams. He collected A's and ninety percents as fervently as he collected honour marks. And what he had just said had stopped all that.

"Exactly," said Nirupam. "Now you've *got* to say it. Nothing I say —"

"Oh, all right. Nothing I say is going to come true in future," Simon said peevishly.

Nirupam let go of him with a sigh of relief and went back to pick up his desk. Everyone sighed. Charles turned sadly away. Well, it had been good while it lasted.

"What's the matter?" Nirupam asked, catching sight of Charles's doleful face as he stood his desk on its legs again.

"Nothing," Charles said. "I – I've got detention."

Then, with a good deal more pleasure, he turned to Simon. "So have you," he said.

Simon was scandalized. "What? I've never had detention all the time I've been at this school!"

It was explained to him that this was untrue. Quite a number of people were surprisingly ready to give Simon details of how he had rendered himself mindless and gained an hour and a half of detention from Mr Crossley. Simon took it in very bad part and stormed off muttering.

Charles was about to trudge away after Simon, when Nirupam caught his arm. "Sit in the back bench," he said. "There's a store of comics in the middle, on the shelf underneath."

"Thanks," said Charles. He was so unused to people being friendly that he said it with enormous surprise and almost forgot to take Mr Towers's awful book with him.

He trudged towards the old lab, where detention was held, and shortly found himself trudging behind Theresa Mullett. Theresa was proceeding towards detention, looking wronged and tragic, supported by a crowd of her friends, with Karen Grigg in addition.

"It's only for an hour," Charles heard Karen say consolingly.

"A whole *hour*!" Theresa exclaimed. "I shall never forgive Teddy Crossley for this! I hope Miss Hodge kicks him in the teeth!"

In order not to go behind Theresa's procession the whole way, Charles turned off halfway through the quadrangle and went by the way that was always called "round the back". It was a grassy space which had once been a second quadrangle. But the new labs and the lecture room and the library had been built in the space, sticking out into the grass at odd angles, so that the space had been pared down to a zig-zag of grassy passage, where, for some reason, there was always a piercing wind blowing. It was a place where people only went to keep out of the way. So Charles was not particularly surprised to see Nan Pilgrim loitering about there. He prepared to glare at her as he trudged by. But Nan got in first with a very unfriendly look and moved off round the library corner.

I'm glad it wasn't Charles Morgan who wrote me that note, Nan thought, as Charles went on without speaking. I don't want any help from *him*.

She loitered out into the keen wind again, wondering if she needed help from anyone. She still felt a strong, confident inner witchiness. It was marvellous. It was like laughter bubbling up through everything she thought. She could not believe that it might be only Simon's doing. On the other hand, no one knew better than Nan how quickly inner confidence could drain away. Particularly if someone like Theresa laughed at you.

Another person was coming. Brian Wentworth this time. But he scurried by on the other side of the passage, to Nan's relief. She did not think Brian could help anyone. And – this place seemed unusually popular this evening – here was Nirupam Singh now, wandering up from the other direction, looking rather pleased with himself.

"I took the spell off Simon Silverson," he said to Nan. "I got him to say nothing he said was true."

"Good," said Nan. She wandered away round the library corner again. Did this mean she was no longer a witch then? She poked with one foot at the leaves and crisp packets the wind had blown into the corner. She could test it by turning them into something, she supposed.

But Nirupam had followed her round the corner. "No, wait," he said. "It was me that sent you that note."

Nan found this extremely embarrassing. She pretended to be very interested in the dead leaves. "I don't need help," she said gruffly.

Nirupam smiled and leant against the library wall as if he was sunning himself. Nirupam had rather a strong

108

personality, Nan realized. Though the sun was thin and yellow and the wind was whirling crisp packets about, Nirupam gave out such a strong impression of basking that Nan almost felt warm. "Everyone thinks you're a witch," he said.

"Well I *am*," Nan insisted, because she wanted to be sure of it herself.

"You shouldn't admit it," said Nirupam. "But it makes no difference. The point is, it's only a matter of time before someone goes to Miss Cadwallader and accuses you."

"Are you sure? They all want me to do things," said Nan.

"Theresa doesn't," said Nirupam. "Besides, you can't please everybody. Someone will get annoyed before long. I know this, because my brother tried to please all the servants. But one of them thought my brother was giving more to the other servants and told the police. And my brother was burnt in the streets of Delhi."

"I'm sorry – I didn't know," said Nan. She looked across at Nirupam. His profile was like a chubby hawk, she thought. It looked desperately sad.

"My mother was burnt too, for trying to save him" Nirupam said. "That was why my father came to this country, but things are just the same here. What I want to tell you is this – I have heard of a witches' underground rescue service in England. They help accused witches to escape, if you can get to one of their branches before the Inquisitors come. I don't know where they send you, or who to ask, but Estelle does. If you are accused, you must get Estelle to help."

"Estelle?" Nan said. She thought of Estelle's soft brown eyes and soft wriggly curls, and of Estelle's irritating chatter, and of Estelle's even more irritating way of imitating Theresa. She could not see Estelle helping anyone.

"Estelle is rather nice," said Nirupam. "I come round

here and talk to her quite often."

"You mean Estelle talks to *you*," said Nan.

Nirupam grinned. "She does talk a lot," he agreed. "But she will help. She told me she likes you. She was sad you didn't like her."

Nan gaped. Estelle? It was not possible. No one liked Nan. But, now she remembered, Estelle had refused to come and threaten to drown her in the bathroom. "All right," she said. "I'll ask her. Thanks. But are you *sure* I'll be accused?"

Nirupam nodded. "There is this, you see. There are at least two other witches in 2Y —"

"Two?" said Nan. "I mean, I know there's *one* more. It's obvious. But why *two*?"

"I told you," said Nirupam, "I've had experience of witches. Each one has their own style. It's like the way everyone's writing is different. And I tell you that it was not the same person who did the birds in Music and the spell on Simon today. Those are two quite different outlooks on life. But both those people must know they have been very silly to do anything at all, and they will both be wanting to put the blame on you. It could well be one of them who accuses you. So you must be very careful. I will do my part and warn you if I hear of any trouble coming. Then you must ask Estelle to help you. Do you see now?"

"Yes, and I'm awfully grateful," said Nan. Regretfully, she saw she did not dare try turning the dead leaves into anything. And, in spite of her promise to the old broom, she had better not ride it again. She was quite frightened. Yet she still felt the laughing confidence bubbling up inside, even though there might not be anything now to be confident about. Watch it! she told herself. You must be mad!

Chapter Nine

The old lab was not used for anything much except detention. But there was still a faint smell of old science clinging to it, from generations of experiments which had gone wrong. Charles slid into the splintery back bench and propped Mr Towers's awful book against the stump of an old gas-pipe. The comics were there, stacked on the shelf underneath, just below a place where someone had spent industrious hours carving *Cadwallader is a bag* on the bench top. The rest of the people in the room were all at the front. They were mostly from 1X or 1Z, and probably did not know about the comics.

Simon came in. Charles gave him a medium-strength glare to discourage him from the back bench. Simon went and sat haughtily in the very middle of the middle bench. Good. Then Mr Wentworth came in. Not so good. Mr Wentworth was carefully carrying a steaming mug of coffee, which everyone in the room looked at with mute envy. It would *have* to be Mr Wentworth! Charles thought resentfully.

Mr Wentworth set his cup of coffee carefully down on the master's bench and looked round to see who was doing time. He seemed surprised to see Simon and not at all surprised to see Charles. "Anyone need paper for lines?" he asked.

Charles did. He went up with most of 1X and was handed a lump of someone's old exam. The exam had only used one side of the paper, so, Charles supposed, it made sense to use the other side for lines. But it did, all

111

the same, seem like a deliberate way of showing people how pointlessly they were wasting time here. Wasting waste-paper. And Charles could tell, as Mr Wentworth gave the paper out, that he was in his nastiest and most harrowed mood.

Not good at all, Charles thought, as he slid back behind the back bench. For, though Charles had not particularly thought about it, it was obvious to him that he was going to use witchcraft to copy out Mr Towers's awful book. What was the point of being a witch if you didn't make use of it? But he would have to go carefully with Mr Wentworth in this mood.

The door opened. Theresa made an entry with her crowd of supporters.

Mr Wentworth looked at them. "Come in," he said. "So glad you were able to make it, all of you. Sit down, Delia. Find a seat, Karen. Heather, Deborah, Julia, Theresa and the rest can no doubt all squeeze in round Simon."

"*We* haven't got detention, sir," Delia said.

"We just came to bring Theresa," Deborah explained.

"Why? Didn't she know the way?" said Mr Wentworth. "Well, you all have detention now—"

"But, sir! We only came—!"

"—unless you get out this second," said Mr Wentworth.

Theresa's friends vanished. Theresa looked angrily at Simon, who was sitting in the place she would otherwise have chosen, and carefully selected a place at the end of the bench just behind him. "This is all your fault," she whispered to Simon.

"Drop dead!" said Simon.

It was, Charles thought, rather a pity that Nirupam had managed to break the *Simon Says* spell.

Silence descended, the woeful, restless silence of people who wish they were elsewhere. Mr Wentworth opened a book and picked up his coffee. Charles waited until Mr Wentworth seemed thoroughly into his book, and then brought out his ballpoint pen. He ran his finger and thumb down it, just as he had done with Simon's hair, down and down again. Write lines, he thought to it. Write five hundred lines out of this book. Write lines. Then, very grudgingly, he wrote out the first sentence for it — *"What ripping fun!" exclaimed Watts Minor. "I'm down for scrum half this afternoon!"* — to show it what to do. Then he cautiously let go of it. And the pen not only stood where he had left it but began to write industriously. Charles arranged Mr Towers's book so that it would hide the scribbling pen. Then, with a sigh of satisfaction, he fetched out one of the comics and settled down as comfortably as Mr Wentworth.

Five minutes later, he thought a thunderbolt hit him.

The pen fell down and rolled on the floor. The comic was snatched away. His right ear was in agony. Charles looked up — mistily, because his glasses were now hanging from his left ear — to find Mr Wentworth towering over him. The pain in his ear was from the excruciatingly tight grip Mr Wentworth had on it.

"Get up," Mr Wentworth said, dragging at the ear.

Charles got up perforce. Mr Wentworth led him, like that, by the ear, with his head painfully on one side, to the front of the room. Halfway there, Charles's glasses fell off his other ear. He almost had not the heart to catch them. In fact, he only saved them by reflex. He was fairly sure he would not be needing them much longer.

At the front, he could see just well enough to watch Mr Wentworth cram the comic one-handed into the wastepaper basket. "Let that teach you to read comics in detention!" Mr Wentworth said. "Now come with me." He led Charles, still by the ear, to the door. There, he turned round and spoke to the others in the room. "If anyone so much as stirs," he said, "while I'm gone, he or she will be here for double the time, every night till Christmas." Upon this, he towed Charles outside.

113

He towed Charles some distance up the covered way outside. Then he let go of Charles's ear, took hold of his shoulders, and commenced shaking him. Charles had never been shaken like it. He bit his tongue. He thought his neck was breaking. He thought the whole of him was coming apart. He grabbed his left hand in his right one to try and hold himself together – and felt his glasses snap into two pieces. That was it, then. He could hardly breathe when Mr Wentworth at last let go of him.

"I warned you!" Mr Wentworth said, furiously angry. "I called you to my room and purposely warned you! Are you a complete fool, boy? How much more frightened do you have to be? Do you need to be in front of the Inquisitors before you stop?"

"I—" gasped Charles. "I—" He had never known Mr Wentworth could be this angry.

Mr Wentworth went on, in a lifting undertone that was far more frightening than shouting, "Three times – three times today to *my* knowledge – you've used witchcraft. And the Lord knows how many times I *don't* know about. Are you *trying* to give yourself away? Have you the *least* idea what risk you run? What kind of a show-off are you? *All* the shoes in the school this morning—"

"That – that was a mistake, sir," Charles panted. "I – I was trying to find my spikes."

"A *stupid* thing to waste witchcraft on!" said Mr Wentworth. "And not content with a public display like that, you *then* go and cast spells on Simon Silverson!"

"How did you know that was me?" said Charles.

"One look at your face, boy. And what's more, you were sitting there letting the unfortunate Nan Pilgrim take the blame. I call that thoroughly selfish and despicable! And now this! Writing lines where anyone could see you! You are lucky, let me tell you, boy, *very* lucky not to be down at the police station at this moment, waiting for the Inquisitor. You *deserve* to be there. Don't you?" He shook Charles again. "Don't you?"

"Yes, sir," said Charles.

"And you will be," said Mr Wentworth, "if you do one more thing. You're to forget about witchcraft, understand? Forget about magic. Try to be normal, if you know what that means. Because I promise you that if you do it again, you will be *really* in trouble. Is that clear?"

"Yes, sir," said Charles.

"Now get back in there and write properly!" Mr Wentworth shoved Charles in front with one hand, and Charles could feel that hand shaking with anger. Frightening though that was, Charles was glad of it. He could barely scc a thing without his glasses. When Mr Wentworth burst back with him into the old lab, the room was just a large fuzzy blur. But he could tell everyone was looking at him. The air was thick with people thinking, I'm glad it wasn't me!

"Get back to your seat," Mr Wentworth said, and let go of Charles with a sharp push.

Charles felt his way through swimming coloured blurs, down to the other end of the old lab. Those crooked white squares must be the book and the old exam paper. But his pen, he remembered, had fallen on the floor. How was he to find it, in this state, let alone write with it?

"What are you standing there for?" Mr Wentworth barked at him. "Put your glasses on and get back to work!"

Charles jumped with terror. He found himself diving for his seat, and hooking his glasses on as he dived. The world clicked into focus. He saw his pen lying almost under his feet and bent to pick it up. But surely, he thought, as he was half under the bench, his glasses had been in two pieces? He had heard a dreadfully final snapping noise. He thought he had felt them come apart. He put his hand up hurriedly and felt his glasses – there was no point taking them off and looking, because then

115

he would not be able to see. They felt all right. Entire and whole. Either he had made a mistake, or the plastic had snapped and not the metal inside. Much relieved, Charles sat up with the pen in his hand.

And stared at what it had written by itself. *I am Watts down scrum Minor ripping this fun afternoon. I fun Minor am half this afternoon Watts ...* and so on, for two whole pages. It was no good. Mr Towers was bound to notice. Charles sighed and began writing. Perhaps he *should* stop doing witchcraft. Nothing seemed to go right.

Consequently, the rest of the evening was rather quiet. Charles sat in devvy running his thumb over the fat cushion of blister on his finger, not wanting to give up witchcraft and knowing he dared not go on. He felt such a mixture of regret and terror that it quite bewildered him. Simon was subdued too. Brian Wentworth was back, sitting scribbling industriously, with one eye still turned slightly inwards, but Simon seemed to have lost his desire to hit Brian for the time being. And Simon's friends followed Simon's lead.

Nan kept quiet also, because of what Nirupam had said, but, however hard she reasoned with herself, she could not get rid of that bubbling inner confidence. It was still with her in the dormitory that night. It stayed, in spite of Delia, Deborah, Heather and the rest, who began on her in their usual way.

"It was a bit much, that spell on Simon!"

"Really, Nan, I know we asked you, but you should *think* first."

"Look what he did to Theresa. And she lost her knitting over it."

And Nan, instead of submitting or apologizing, as she usually did, said, "What's put it into your pretty little heads that that spell was mine?"

"Because we know you're a witch," said Heather.

"Of course," said Nan. "But what gave you the idea I

116

was the only one? You think, Heather, instead of just opening your little pink mouth and letting words trickle out. I told you, it takes *time* to make a spell. I told you about picking herbs and flying round and chanting, didn't I? And I left out the way you have to catch bats. That takes ages, even on a fast modern broomstick, because bats are so good at dodging. And you were with me in the bathroom, and with me all the time all this last week, and you *know* I haven't had time to catch bats or pick herbs, and you've *seen* I haven't been muttering and incantating. So you see? It wasn't me."

She could tell they were convinced, because they all looked so disappointed. Heather muttered, "And you said you couldn't fly that broomstick!" but she said nothing more. Nan was pleased. She seemed to have shut them up without losing her reputation as a witch.

All except Karen. Karen was newly admitted to the number of Theresa's friends. That made her very zealous. "Well I think you should work a spell now," she said. "Theresa's lost a pair of bootees she spent hours knitting, and I think the least you can do is get them back for her."

"No trouble at all," Nan said airily. "But does Theresa want me to try?"

Theresa finished buttoning her pyjamas and turned away to brush her hair. "She's not going to try, Karen," she said. "I should be *ashamed* to get my knitting back that way!"

"Lights out," said a prefect at the door. "Do these belong to anyone? The caretaker found them in his dog's basket." She held up two small grey fluffy things with holes in.

The look everyone gave Nan, as Theresa went to claim her bootees, made Nan wonder if she had been wise to talk like that. And I don't even really know if I'm still a witch, she thought, as she got into bed. I'll keep my mouth shut in future. And that broomstick stays on top

117

of the cupboard. I don't care if I did promise it.

Right in the middle of the night, she was woken by something prodding at her. Nan, in her sleep, rolled out of the way, and rolled again, until she woke up in the act of falling out of bed. There was a swift swishing noise. Something she only dimly saw in the near-dark dived over her and then dived under her. Nan woke up completely to find herself six feet off the floor and doubled over the broomstick, with her head hanging down one side and her feet the other. The knobby handle was a painful thing to be draped over. Nevertheless, Nan began to laugh. I *am* a witch after all! she thought joyfully.

"Put me down, you big fraud!" she whispered. "You were just playing for sympathy, pretending you needed a rider, weren't you? Put me down and go and fly yourself!"

The broomstick's answer was to rise up to the ceiling. Nan's bed looked a small dim oblong from there. She knew she would miss it if she tried to jump off.

"You big bully!" she said. "I know I promised, but that was before—"

The broom drifted suggestively towards the window. Nan became alarmed. The window was open because Theresa believed in fresh air. She had visions of herself being carted over the countryside, draped over the stick in nothing but pyjamas. She gave in.

"All right. I'll fly you. But let me go down and get some blankets first. I'm not going to go like this!"

The broom whirled round and swooped back to Nan's bed. Nan's legs flew out and she landed on the mattress with a bounce. The broom did not trust her in the least. It hovered over her while she dragged the pink school blankets from her bed, and as soon as she had wrapped them round her, it made quite sure of her by darting underneath her and swooping up to the ceiling again. Nan was thrown backwards. She nearly ended hanging

118

underneath again.

"Go carefully!" she whispered. "Let me get settled."

The broom hovered impatiently while Nan tried to balance herself and get comfortable. She did not dare take too long over it. All the swooping and whispering was disturbing the other girls. Quite a few of them were turning over and murmuring crossly. Nan tried to sit on the broom and toppled over sideways. She got tangled in her blankets. In the end, she simply fell forward on her face and settled for lying along the handle again, in a bundle of blanket, with her feet hooked up on the brush.

Before she had even got comfortable like that, the broomstick swooped to the window, nudged it further open, and darted outside. There was pitch black night out there. It was cold, with a drizzle of rain falling. Nan wrinkled her face against it and tried to get used to being high up. The broom flew with a strange choppy movement, not altogether pleasant for a person lying on her face.

Nan talked, to take her mind off it. "How is this," she said, "for romantic dreams come true? I always thought of myself flying a broomstick on a warm summer night, outlined against an enormous moon, with a nightingale or so singing its head off. And look at us!" Underneath her, the broomstick jerked. It was obviously a shrug.

"Yes, I daresay it is the best we can do," Nan said. "But I don't feel very glamorous like this, and I'm getting wet. I bet Dulcinea Wilkes used to *sit* on her broom, gracefully, sidesaddle probably, with her long hair flowing out behind. And because it was London, she probably wore an elegant silk dress, with lots of lacy pet-ticoats showing from underneath. Did you know I was descended from Dulcinea Wilkes?"

The rippling underneath her might have been the broom's way of nodding. But it could have been laughing at the contrast.

Nan found she could see in the dark now. She looked

119

down and blenched. The broomstick felt very flimsy to be this high. It had soared and turned while she was talking, so that the square shapes of the school were a long way below and to one side. The pale spread of the playing field was directly underneath, and beyond that Nan could see the entire town, filling the valley ahead. The houses were all dark, with orange chains of street lights in between. And in spite of the drifting drizzle, Nan could see as far as the blackness of Larwood Forest on the hill opposite.

"Let's fly over the forest," she said.

The broom swept off. Once you got used to it, it really would be a nice feeling, Nan told herself firmly, blinking against the drizzle. Secret, silent flight. It was in her blood. She held the end of the broom handle in both hands and tried to point it at the town. But the broom had other ideas. It wanted to go round the edge of the town. The result was that they flew sideways, jolting a little.

"Fly over the houses," said Nan.

The broom gave a shake that nearly sent her tumbling off. No.

"I suppose someone might look up and see us," Nan agreed. 'All right. You win again. Bully." And it occurred to her that her dreams of flying against a huge full moon were really the most arrant romantic nonsense. No witch in her senses would do that, for fear the Inquisitors saw her.

So they swooped over fields and across the main road in a rush of rain. The rain at first came at Nan's face in separate drops out of the orange haze made by the street lights. Then it was just wetness out of darkness, as they reached Larwood Forest, and the wetness brought a smell with it of autumn leaves and mushroom. But even a dark wood is not quite black at night. Nan could see paler trees, which still had yellow leaves, and she could clearly see mist caused by the rain smoking out above the trees. Some of it seemed to be real smoke. Nan smelt fire, distinctly. A wet fire, burning smokily.

She suddenly felt rather quiet. "I say, that can't be a bone-fire, can it? If it's after midnight, it is Hallowe'en, isn't it?"

The idea seemed to upset the broom. It stopped with a jerk. For a second, its front end tipped downwards as if it were thinking of landing. Nan had to grip hard in order not slide off head first. Then it began actually flying backwards, wagging its brush in agitated sweeps, so that Nan's feet were swirled from side to side.

"Stop it!" she said. "I shall be sick in a minute!"

They did, she knew, sometimes burn witch's brooms with the witch they belonged to. So she was not surprised when the broom swung round, away from the smell of smoke, and began flying back towards the school, in a stately sort of way, as if that was the way it had meant to go all along.

"You don't fool me," she said. "But you can go back if you want. I'm soaked."

The broom continued on its wet and stately way, high above the fields and the main road, until the pale flatness of the playing field appeared beneath them once more. Nan was just thinking that she would be in bed any minute now, when a new notion seemed to strike the broom. It dived a sickening fifty feet and put on speed. Nan found herself hurtling over the field, about twenty feet up, and oozing off backwards with the speed. She hung on and shouted to it to stop. Nothing she said made any difference. The broom continued to hurtle.

"Oh really!" Nan gasped. "You are the most wilful thing I've ever known! Stop!"

The rain beat in her face, but she could see something ahead now, all the same. It was something dark against the grass, and it was quite big, too big for a broom, although it was flying too, floating gently away across the field. The broom was racing towards it. As they

121

plunged on, Nan saw that the thing was flat underneath, with the shape of a person on top of it. It got bigger and bigger. Nan decided it could only be a small carpet with a man sitting on it. She tugged and jerked at the broom handle, but there seemed nothing she could do to stop the broom.

The broom plunged gladly up alongside the dark shape. It *was* a man on a small carpet. The broom swooped round it, wagging its end so hard that Nan bit her tongue. It nuzzled and nudged and jogged at the carpet, jerking Nan this way and that as it went. And the carpet seemed equally delighted to meet the broom. It was jiggling and flapping, and rippling so that the man on top of it was rolled this way and that. Nan shrank down and clung to the broom, hoping that she just looked like a roll of blankets to whoever this witch on a carpet was.

But the man was becoming annoyed by the antics of the carpet and the broom. "Can't you control that thing yet?" he snapped.

Nan shrank down even further. Her bitten tongue made it hard to speak anyway, and she was almost glad of it. She knew that voice. It was Mr Wentworth's.

"And I told you never to ride that thing in term time, Brian," Mr Wentworth said. When Nan still did not say anything, he added, "I know, I know. But this wretched hearthrug insists on going out every night."

This is worse and worse! Nan thought. Mr Wentworth thought she was Brian. So Brian must be – with a fierce effort, she managed to wrench the broom round, away from the hearthrug. With an even fiercer effort, she got it going again, towards the school. By kicking it hard with her bare toes, she kept it going. When she was some way away, she risked turning round and whispering, "Sorry." She hoped Mr Wentworth would go on thinking she was Brian.

Mr Wentworth called something after her as the

broomstick lumbered away, but Nan did not even try to hear what it was. She did not want to know. She could still barely believe it. Besides, she needed all her attention to make the broom go. It was very reluctant. It flew across the field in a dismal, trudging way, which reminded Nan irresistibly of Charles Morgan, but at least it went. Nan was pleased to discover that she could control it after all, when she had to.

It made particularly heavy weather of lifting Nan upwards to her dormitory window. She almost believed it groaned. Some of the difficulty may have been real. All Nan's pink school blankets were soaked through by now and they must have weighed a great deal. But Nan remembered what an act the broom had put on in the afternoon and resolved to be pitiless. She drummed with her toes again. Up went the broom through the dark rainy night, up and up the wall, until at last they were outside the half-open dormitory window. Nan helped the broom shoulder the window open wider, and then swooped to the floor on her stomach. What a relief! she thought.

Someone whispered, "I put dry blankets on your bed."

Nan nearly fainted. After a pause to recover, she rolled herself off the broom and knelt up in her sopping blankets. A dim figure in regulation school pyjamas was standing in front of her, bending down a little, so that Nan could see the hair was curly. Heather? No, don't be daft! Estelle. "Estelle?" she whispered.

"Hush!" whispered Estelle. "Come and help put these blankets in the airing cupboard. We can talk there."

"But the broom—?" Nan whispered.

"Send it away."

A good idea, Nan thought, if only the broom would obey. She picked it up, shedding soaking blankets as she went, and carried it to the window. "Go to the grounds-man's shed," she told it in a severe whisper, and sent it off with a firm shove. Knowing the kind of broom it was, she would not have been surprised if it had simply clattered to the ground. But it obeyed her, rather to her astonishment – or at least, it flew off into the rainy night.

Estelle was already lugging the heap of blankets to the door. Nan tiptoed to help her. Together they dragged the heap down the passage and into the fateful bathroom. There, Estelle shut the door and daringly turned on the light.

"It'll be all right if we don't talk too loud," she said. "I'm awfully sorry – Theresa woke up while I was making your bed. I had to tell her you'd been sick. I said you were in the loo being sick again. Can you remember that if she asks tomorrow?"

"Thanks," said Nan. "That was kind of you. Did I wake you going out?"

"Yes, but it was training mostly," Estelle said. She opened the big airing cupboard. "If we fold these blankets and put them right at the back, no one's going to find them for weeks. They might even be dry by then, but with this school's heating there's no relying on that."

It was not a quick job. They had to take out the piles of pale pink dry blankets stacked in the cupboard, fold the heavy bright pink wet ones, put them in at the back, and then put all the dry ones back to hide them.

"Why did you say training woke you up?" Nan asked Estelle as they worked.

"Training with the witches' underground escape route," said Estelle. "My mum used to belong to it, and I used to help her. It took me right back, when I heard you going out – though it was usually people coming in that used to wake me up. And I knew you'd be wet when you came back, and need help. Mum brought me up to think of everything like that. We used to have witches coming in on brooms at all hours of the night, poor things. Most of them were as wet as you – and much more frightened of course. Hold the blanket down with your chin. That's the best way to get it folded."

"Why did your mum send you away to this school?" Nan asked. "You must have been such a help."

Estelle's bright face saddened. "She didn't. The Inquisitors sent me. They had a big campaign and broke up all our branch of the organization. My mum got caught. She's in prison now, for helping witches. But," Estelle's soft brown eyes looked earnestly into Nan's face, *"please* don't say. I couldn't bear anyone else to know. You're the only one I've ever told."

Chapter Ten

The next morning, Brian Wentworth did not get up. Simon threw a pillow at him as he lay there, but Brian did not stir.

"Wakey, wakey, Brian!" Simon said. "Get up, or I'll strip your bed off." When Brian still did not move, Simon advanced on his bed.

"Let him alone," Charles said. "He was ill yesterday."

"Anything you say, Charles," said Simon. "Your word is my command." And he pulled all the covers off Brian's bed.

Brian was not in it. Instead, there was a line of three pillows, artfully overlapped to give the shape of a body. Everyone gathered round and stared. Ronald West bent down and looked under the bed – as if he thought Brian might be there – and came up holding a piece of paper.

"Here," he said. "This must have come off with the bedclothes. Take a look!"

Simon snatched the paper from him. Everyone else craned and pushed to see it too. It was written in capital letters, in ordinary blue ballpoint, and it said: *HA HA. I HAVE GOT BRIAN WENTWORTH IN MY POWER. SIGNED, THE WITCH.*

The slightly tense look on Simon's face gave way to righteous concern. He had known at once that Brian's disappearance had nothing to do with him. "We're not going to panic," he said. "Someone get the master on duty."

There was instant emergency. Voices jabbered,

rumours roared. Charles fetched Mr Crossley, since everyone else seemed too astonished to think. After that, Mr Crossley and prefects came and went, asking everyone when they had last seen Brian. People from the other dormitories crowded in the doorway, calling comments. Everyone was very eager to say something, but nothing very useful came out. A lot of people had noticed Brian was pale and cross-eyed the day before. Somebody said he had been ill and gone to Matron. A number of other people said he had come back later and seemed very busy writing. Everyone swore Brian had gone to bed as usual the night before.

Long before Mr Crossley had sorted even this much out, Charles was tiptoeing hastily away downstairs. He felt sick. Up to last night, he had supposed Brian was trying to get himself invalided out of school. Now he knew better. Brian had run away, just as he had said he would. And he had taken the advice Charles had given him in the middle of the night before and confused his trail. But what had given Brian the idea of blaming the witch? Could it have been the shoes, and the sight of Charles muttering over some hairs from Simon's comb? Charles was fairly sure it was.

As Charles pushed through the boys in the corridor, he heard the words "witch" and "Nan Pilgrim" coming from all sides. Fine, as long as they went on blaming Nan. But would they? Charles took a look at his burnt finger as he went down the stairs. The transparent juicy cushion of blister on it was fatter than ever. *It hurts to be burnt*. Charles went the rest of the way down at a crazy gallop. He too remembered Brian scribbling and scribbling during devvy. Brian must have written pages. If there was one word about Charles Morgan in those pages, he was going to make sure no one else saw them. He pelted along the corridors. He flung himself into the classroom, squawking for breath.

Brian's desk was open. Nirupam was bending over it.

He did not seem in the least surprised to see Charles. "Brian has been very eloquent," he said. "Come and see."

Behind the raised lid of the desk, Nirupam had lined up six exercise books, each of them open to a double page of hurried blue scrawl. *Help, help, help, help,* Charles read in the first. *The witch has the Evil Eye on me. HELP. I am being dragged away I know not where. HELP. My mind is in thrall. Nameless deeds are being forced upon me. HELP. The world is turning grey. The spell is working. Help*... And so on, for the whole two pages.

"There's yards of it!" said Charles.

"I know," said Nirupam, opening Brian's French book. "This is full of it too."

"Does he give names?" Charles asked tensely.

"Not so far," said Nirupam.

Charles was not going to take Nirupam's word for that. He picked up each book in turn and read the scrawl through. *Help. Wild chanting and horrible smells fill my ears. HELP. I can FEEL MYSELF GOING. The witch's will is strong. I must obey. Grey humming and horrible words. HELP. My spirit is being dragged from TIMBUKTU to UTTAR PRADESH. To utter destruction I mean. Help*... It went on like this for all six books. Enough of it was in capitals for Charles to be quite sure that Brian had written the note in his bed himself.

After that, he read each of the rest of Brian's books as Nirupam finished with it. It was all the same kind of thing. To Charles's relief, Brian named no names. But there was still Brian's journal, at the bottom of the pile.

"If he's said anything definite, it will be in this," Nirupam said, picking up the journal. Charles reached out for it too. If necessary, he was going to force it out of Nirupam's hands by witchcraft. Or was it better just to make all the pages blank? But did he dare do either? His hand hesitated.

As Charles hesitated, they heard Mr Crossley's voice out in the corridor. Charles and Nirupam frantically crammed the books back into Brian's desk and shut it. They raced to their own desks, sat down, got out books, and pretended to be busy finishing devvy from the night before.

"You boys should be going along to breakfast now," Mr Crossley said, when he came in. "Go along."

Both of them had to go, without a chance of looking at Brian's journal. Charles wondered why Nirupam looked so frustrated. But he was too frightened on his own account to bother much about Nirupam's feelings.

In the corridor outside the dining hall, Mr Wentworth rushed past them, looking even more harrowed than usual. Inside the dining hall, the rumour was going round that the police had just arrived.

"You wait," Simon said knowingly. "The Inquisitor will be here before dinner time. You'll see."

Nirupam slid into a seat beside Nan. "Brian has written in all his school books about a witch putting a spell on him," he murmured to her.

Nan hardly needed this to show her the trouble she was in. Karen and Delia had already asked her several times what she had done to Brian. And Theresa had added, not looking at Nan, "Some people can't leave people alone, can they?"

"But he didn't name any names," Nirupam muttered, also not looking at Nan.

Brian didn't need to name names, Nan thought desperately. Everyone else would do that for him. And, if that was not enough, Estelle knew she had been out on the broomstick last night. She looked round for Estelle, but Estelle seemed to be avoiding her. She was at another table. At that, the last traces of witchy inner confidence

129

left Nan completely. For once in her life, she had no appetite for breakfast. Charles was not much better. Whatever he tried to eat, the fat blister on his finger seemed to get in the way.

At the end of breakfast, another rumour went round: the police had sent for tracker dogs.

A short while after this, Miss Hodge arrived, to find the school in an uproar. It took her some time to find out what had happened, since Mr Crossley was nowhere to be found. When Miss Phillips finally told her, Miss Hodge was delighted. Brian Wentworth had vanished! That is, Miss Hodge thought hastily, it was very sad and worrying of course, but it did give her a real excuse to attract Mr Wentworth's attention again. Yesterday had been most frustrating. After Mr Wentworth had brushed aside her generous apology over Charles Morgan, she had not been able to think of any other move towards getting him to marry her. But this was ideal. She could go to Mr Wentworth and be terribly sympathetic. She could enter into his sorrow. The only difficulty was that Mr Wentworth was not to be found, any more than Mr Crossley. It seemed that they were both with the police in Miss Cadwallader's study.

As everyone went into the hall for assembly, they could see a police van in the quadrangle. Several healthy Alsatians were getting out of it, with their pink tongues draped over their large white fangs in a way that suggested they could hardly wait to get on and hunt something. A number of faces turned pale. There was a lot of nervous giggling.

"It doesn't matter if the dogs don't find anything," Simon could be heard explaining. "The Inquisitor will simply run his witch-detector over everyone in the class, and they'll find the witch that way."

To Nan's relief, Estelle came pushing along the line and stood next to her. "Estelle—!" Nan began violently.

"Not now," Estelle whispered. "Wait for the singing."

Neither Mr Wentworth nor Miss Cadwallader came into assembly. Mr Brubeck and Mr Towers, who sat in the main chairs instead, did not explain about that, and neither of them mentioned Brian. This seemed to make it all much more serious. Mr Towers chose his favourite hymn. It was, to Nan's misery, "He who would valiant be". This hymn always caused Theresa to look at Nan and giggle, when it came to "To be a pilgrim". Nan had to wait for Theresa to do that before she dared to speak to Estelle, and, she thought, Theresa's giggle was rather nastier than usual.

"Estelle," Nan whispered, as soon as everyone had started the second verse. "Estelle, you don't think I went out – last night, the way I did – because of Brian, do you? I swear I didn't."

"I know you didn't," Estelle whispered back. "What would anyone want Brian *for*, anyway?"

"But everyone thinks I did! What shall I *do*?" Nan whispered back.

"It's PE second lesson. I'll show you then," said Estelle.

Charles was also whispering under cover of the singing, to Nirupam. "What are witch-detectors? Do they work?"

"Machines in black boxes," Nirupam said breathily at his hymn book. "And they always find a witch with them."

Mr Wentworth had talked about witch-detectors too. So, Charles thought, if the rumour was right and the Inquisitor got here before lunch time, today was the end of Charles. Charles hated Brian. Selfish beast. Yes, all right, he had been selfish too, but Brian was even worse. There was only one thing to do now, and that was to run away as well. But those tracker dogs made that nearly impossible.

When they got to the classroom, Brian's desk had been taken away. Charles looked at the empty space in horror. Fingerprints! he thought. Nirupam had gone quite yellow.

"They took it to give the dogs the scent," said Dan Smith. He added thoughtfully, "They're trained to tear people to pieces, those police dogs. I wonder if they'll tear Brian up, or just the witch."

Charles looked at the blister on his finger and realized that burning was not the only thing that hurt. His first thought had been to run away during break. Now he decided to go in PE, next lesson. He wished there was not a whole lesson in between.

That lesson seemed to last about a year. And for most of that lesson, policemen were continually going past the windows with dogs on leads. Back and forth they went. Wherever Brian had gone, they seemed to be finding it hard to pick up his scent.

By this time, Nan's hands were shaking so that she could hardly hold her pen. Thanks to last night, she knew exactly why Brian had left no scent. It was that double-dealing broomstick. It must have flown Brian out before it came and woke her up. Nan was sure of it. She could have taken the police to the exact spot where Brian was. That was no bone-fire she had smelt over Larwood Forest last night. It had been Brian's camp-fire. The broomstick had brought her right over the spot and then realized its mistake. That was why it had got so agitated and tried to fly away backwards. She was so angry with Brian for getting her blamed that she wished she really could tell them where he was. But the moment she did that, she proved that she was a witch and incriminated Mr Wentworth into the bargain. Oh, it was too bad of Brian! Nan just hoped Estelle could think of some kind of rescue before someone accused her, and she started accusing Brian and Mr Wentworth.

Just before the end of that lesson, the dogs must have found some kind of scent. When the girls walked round the outside of the school on their way to the girls' locker room, to change for PE, there was not a policeman or a dog in sight. As the line of girls went past the shrubbery, Estelle gently took hold of Nan's arm and pulled her towards the bushes. Nan let herself be pulled. She did not know if she was more relieved or more terrified. It was a little early in the day to find seniors in the shrubbery, but even so, surely somebody would notice?

"We have to go into town,' Estelle whispered, as they pushed among the wet bushes. "To the Old Gate House,"

"Why?" Nan asked, thrusting her way after Estelle.

"Because," Estelle whispered over her shoulder, "the lady there runs the Larwood branch of the witches' escape route."

They came out into the grass beside the huge laurel bush. Nan looked from Estelle's scared face to Estelle's trim blazer and school skirt. Then she looked down at her own plump shape. Different as they were, they were both obviously in Larwood House school uniform. "But if someone sees us in town, they'll report us to Miss Cadwallader."

"I was hoping," Estelle whispered, "that you might be able to change us into ordinary clothes."

Nan realized that the only witchcraft she had ever done was to fly that broom. She had not the least idea how you changed clothes. But Estelle was relying on her and it really was urgent. Feeling an awful fool, Nan held out both shaking hands and said the first thing remotely like a spell that came into her head.

"Eeny, meeny, miney, mo,
Out of uniform we go!"

There was a swirling feeling around her. Estelle was suddenly in a small snowstorm that seemed to be made of little bits of rag. Navy blue rag, then dark rag. The rags settled like burnt paper, clinging to Estelle and hanging, and clinging to Nan too. And there they both were in seconds, dressed as witches, in long trailing black dresses, pointed black hats and all.

Estelle clapped both hands to her mouth to stop a giggle. Nan snorted with laughter. "This won't do! Try again," giggled Estelle.

"What do you want to wear?" Nan asked.

Estelle's eyes shone. "Riding clothes," she whispered ardently. "With a red jumper, please."

Nan stretched out her hands again. Now she knew she could do it, she felt quite confident.

"Agga, tagga, ragga, roast,
Wear the clothes you want the most."

The rag-storm began again. In Estelle's case, it started black and swirled very promisingly into pale brown and red. Around Nan, it seemed to be turning pink. When the storm stopped, there was Estelle, looking very trim and pretty in jodhpurs, red sweater and hard hat, with her legs in shiny boots, pointing at Nan with a riding crop and making helpless bursting noises.

Nan looked down at herself. It seemed that the sort of clothes she wanted most was the dress she had imagined Dulcinea Wilkes wearing to ride her broomstick round London in. She was in a shiny pink silk balldress. The full skirt swept the wet grass. The tight pink bodice left her shoulders bare. It had blue bows up the front and lace in the sleeves. No wonder Estelle was laughing! Pink silk was definitely a mistake for someone as plump as Nan. Why pink? she wondered. Probably she had got that idea from the school blankets.

She had her hands stretched out to try again, when they heard Karen Grigg shouting outside the shrubbery. "Estelle! *Estelle!* Where are you? Miss Phillips wants to know where you've got to!"

Estelle and Nan turned and ran. Estelle's clothes were

ideal for sprinting through bushes. Nan's were not. She lumbered and puffed behind Estelle, and wet leaves kept showering her bare shoulders with water. Her sleeves got in her way. Her skirt wrapped round her legs and kept catching on bushes. Just at the edge of the shrubbery, the dress got stuck on a twig and tore with such a loud ripping noise that Estelle whirled round in horror.

"Wait!" panted Nan. She wrenched the pink skirt loose and tore the whole bottom part of it off. She wrapped the torn bit like a scarf round her wet shoulders. "That's better."

After that, she could keep up with Estelle quite easily. They slipped through on to the school drive and pelted down it and out through the iron gates. Nan meant to stop and change the pink dress into something else in the road outside, but there was a man sweeping the pavement just beyond the gates. He stopped sweeping and stared at the two of them. A little further on, there were two ladies with shopping bags, who stared even harder. Nan put her head down in acute embarrassment as they walked past the ladies. She had strips of torn pink silk hanging down and clinging to the pale blue stockings she seemed to have changed her socks into. Below that, she seemed to have given herself pink ballet shoes.

"Will you call for me at my ballet class after you've had your riding lesson?" she said loudly and desperately to Estelle.

"I might. But I'm scared of your ballet teacher," Estelle said, playing up bravely.

They got past the ladies, but there were more people further down the road. The further they got into town, the more people there were. By the time they came to the shops, Nan knew she was not going to get a chance to change the pink balldress.

"You look awfully pretty. Really," Estelle said consolingly.

"No, I don't. It's like a bad dream," said Nan.

"In my bad dreams like that, I don't have any clothes on at all," said Estelle.

At last they reached the strange red brick castle which was the Old Gate House. Estelle, looking white and nervous, led Nan up the steps and under the pointed porch. Nan pulled the large bell-pull hanging beside the pointed front door. Then they stood under the arch and waited, more nervous than ever.

For a long time, they thought nobody was going to answer the door. Then, after nearly five minutes, it opened, very slowly and creaking a great deal. A very old lady stood there, leaning on a stick, looking at them in some surprise.

Estelle was so nervous by then that she stuttered. "A – a w – way out in the n – name of D – Dulcinea," she said.

"Oh dear!" said the old lady. "My dears, I'm so sorry. The Inquisitors broke up the organization here several years ago. If it wasn't for my age, I'd be in prison now. They come and check up on me every week. I daren't do a thing."

They stood and stared at her in utter dismay.

The old lady saw it. "If it's a real emergency," she said, "I can give you a spell. That's all I can think of. Would you like that?"

They nodded, dismally.

"Then wait a moment, while I write it down," said the old lady. She left the front door open and hobbled aside to a table at one side of the dark old hall. She opened a drawer in it and fumbled out some paper. She searched out a pen. Then she looked across at them. "You know, my dears, in order not to attract attention, you really should look as if you were collecting for charity. I can pretend to be writing you a cheque. Can either of you manage collecting boxes?"

"I can," said Nan. She had almost lost her voice with fright and dismay. She had to cough. She did not dare

136

risk saying spells, standing there on the steps of the old house, up above the busy street. She simply waved a quivering hand and hoped.

Instant weight bore her hand down. A mighty collecting tin dangled from her arm, and another dangled from Estelle's. Each was as big as a tin of paint. Each had a huge red cross on one side and chinked loudly from their nervous trembling.

"That's better," said the old lady, and started, very slowly, to write.

The outsize tins did indeed make Nan and Estelle feel easier while they waited. People passing certainly looked up at them curiously, but most of them smiled when they saw the tins. And they were standing there for quite a long time, because, as well as writing very slowly, the old lady kept calling across to them.

"Do either of you know the Portway Oaks?" she called. They shook their heads. "Pity. You have to go there to say this," said the old lady. "It's a ring of trees just below the forest. I'd better draw you a map then." She drew, slowly. Then she called, "I don't know why they're called the Oaks. Every single tree there is a beech tree." Later still, she called, "Now I'm writing down the way you should pronounce it."

The girls still stood there. Nan was beginning to wonder if the old lady was really in league with the Inquisitors and keeping them there on purpose, when the old lady at last folded up the paper and shuffled back to the front door.

"There you are, my dears. I wish I could do more for you."

Nan took the paper. Estelle produced a bright artificial smile. "Thanks awfully," she said. "What does it do?"

"I'm not sure," said the old lady. "It's been handed down in my family for use in emergencies, but no one has ever used it before. I'm told it's very powerful."

Like many old people, the old lady spoke rather too loudly. Nan and Estelle looked nervously over their shoulders at the street below, but nobody seemed to have heard. They thanked the old lady politely and, when the front door shut, they went drearily back down the steps, lugging their huge collecting tins.

"I suppose we'd better use it," said Estelle. "We daren't go back now."

Chapter Eleven

Charles jogged round the playing field towards the groundsman's hut. He hoped anyone who saw him would think he was out running for PE. For this reason, he had changed into his small sky-blue running shorts before he slipped away. When he had time, he supposed he could transform the shorts into jeans or something. But the important thing at the moment was to get hold of that mangy old besom people had been taunting Nan Pilgrim with the other day. If he got to that before anyone noticed he was missing, he could ride away on it and no dog on earth could pick up his trail.

He reached the hut, in its corner beside the kitchen gardens. He crept round it to its door. At the same moment, Nirupam crept round it from the opposite side, also in sky blue shorts, and stretched out his long arm for the door too. The two of them stared at one another. All sorts of ideas for things to say streamed through Charles's mind, from explaining he was just dodging PE, to accusing Nirupam of kidnapping Brian. In the end, he said none of these things. Nirupam had hold of the door-latch by then.

"Bags I the broomstick," Charles said.

"Only if there are two of them," said Nirupam. His face was yellow with fear. He pulled open the door and dodged into the hut. Charles dived in after him.

There was not even the one old broomstick. There were flowerpots, buckets, an old roller, a new roller, four rakes, two spades, a hoe, and an old wet-mop propped in one of the buckets. And that was all.

"Who took it?" Charles said wildly.

"Nobody brought it back," said Nirupam.

"Oh magic it all!" said Charles. "What shall we *do*?"

"Use something else," said Nirupam. "Or walk." He seized the nearest spade and stood astride it, bending and stretching his great long legs. "Fly," he told the spade. "Go on, fly, magic you!"

Nirupam had the right idea, Charles saw. A witch surely ought to be able to make anything fly. "I should think a rake would fly better," he said, and quickly grabbed hold of the wet-mop for himself. The mop was so old that it had stuck to the bucket. Charles was forced to put one foot on the bucket and pull, before it came loose, and a lot of the head got left behind in the bucket. The result was a stick ending in a scraggly grey stump. Charles seized it and stood astride it. He jumped up and down. "Fly!" he told the mop. "Quick!"

Nirupam threw the spade down and snatched up the hoe. Together they jumped desperately round the hut. "Fly!" they panted. "Fly!"

In an old, soggy, dispirited way, the mop obeyed. It wallowed up about three feet into the air and wove towards the hut door. Nirupam was wailing in despair, when the hoe took off too, with a buck and a rush, as if it did not want to be left behind. Nirupam shot past Charles with his huge legs flailing. "It works!" he panted triumphantly, and went off in another kangaroo bound towards the kitchen gardens.

They were forbidden to go in the kitchen gardens, but it seemed the most secret way out of school. Charles followed Nirupam through the gate and down the gravel path, both of them trying to control their mounts. The mop wallowed and wove. It was like an old, old person, feebly hobbling through the air. The hoe either went by kangaroo surges, or it slanted and trailed its metal end along the path. Nirupam had to stick his feet out in front

140

in order not leave a scent on the ground. His eyes rolled in agony. He kept overtaking Charles and dropping behind. When they got to the wall at the end of the garden, both implements stopped. The mop wallowed about in the air. The hoe jittered its end on the gravel.

"They can't go high enough to get over," said Charles. "Now what?"

That might have been the end of their journey, had not the caretaker's dog been sniffing about in the kitchen gardens and suddenly caught their scent. It came racing down the long path towards them, yapping. The hoe and the mop took off like startled cats. They soared over the wall, with Charles and Nirupam hanging on anyhow, and went bucking off down the fields beyond. They raced towards the main road, the mop surging, the hoe plunging and trailing, clearing hedges by a whisker and missing trees by inches. They did not slow down until they had put three fields between them and the caretaker's dog.

"They must hate that dog as much as we do," Nirupam gasped. "Was it you that did the *Simon Says* spell?"

"Yes," said Charles. "Did you do the birds in Music?"

"No," said Nirupam, much to Charles's surprise. "I did only one thing, and that was secret, but I daren't stay if the Inquisitors are going to bring a witch-detector. They always get you with those."

"What did you do?" said Charles.

"You know that night all our shoes went into the hall," said Nirupam. "Well, we had a feast that night. Dan Smith made me get up the floorboards and get the food out. He says I have no right to be so large and so weak," Nirupam said resentfully, "and I was hating him for it, when I took the boards up and found a pair of running-shoes, with spikes, hidden there with the food. I turned those shoes into a chocolate cake. I knew Dan was so greedy that he would eat it all himself. And he did

141

eat it. He didn't let anyone else have any. You may have noticed that he wasn't quite himself the next day."

So much had happened to Charles that particular day, that he could not remember Dan seeming anything at all. He had not the heart to explain all the trouble Nirupam had caused him. "Those were my spikes," he said sadly. He wobbled along on the mop, rather awed at the thought of iron spikes passing through Dan's stomach. "He must have a digestion like an ostrich!"

"The spikes were turned into cherries," said Nirupam. "The soles were the cream. The shoes as a whole became what is called a Black Forest gâteau."

Here they reached the main road and saw the tops of cars whipping past beyond the hedge. "We'll have to wait for a gap in that traffic," Charles said. "Stop!" he commanded the mop.

"Stop!" Nirupam cried to the hoe.

Neither implement took the slightest notice. Since Charles and Nirupam did not dare put their feet down for fear of leaving a scent for the dogs, they could find no way of stopping at all. They were carried helplessly over the hedge. Luckily, the road was down in a slight dip, and they had just height enough to clear the whizzing cars. Nirupam frantically bent his huge legs up. Charles tried not to let his legs dangle. Horns honked. He saw faces peering up at them, outraged and grinning. Charles suddenly saw how ridiculous they must look, both in their little blue shorts: himself with the disgraceful dirty old mop-head wagging behind him; Nirupam lunging through the air in bunny-hops, with a look of anguish on his face.

Horns were still sounding as they cleared the hedge on the other side of the road.

"Oh help!" gasped Nirupam. "Make for the woods, quick, before somebody gets the police!"

Larwood Forest was only a short hillside away and, luckily, their panic seemed to get through to the mop and the hoe. Both put on speed. The wagging and slewing of the mop nearly threw Charles off. The hoe helped itself along by digging its metal end fiercely into the ground, so that Nirupam went upwards like someone on a pogo-stick, yelping at each leap. Horns were still sounding from the road as first Nirupam, then Charles, reached the trees and plunged in among them. By this time, Nirupam was so far ahead that Charles thought he had lost him. Probably just as well, Charles thought. They might be safer going separate ways. But the mop had other ideas. After dithering a bit, as if it had lost the scent, it set off again at top wallow. Charles was wagged round tree trunks and swayed through prickly under-growth. Finally he was slewed through a bed of nettles. He yelled. Nirupam yelled too, just beyond the nettles. The hoe tipped him off into a blackberry bush and darted gladly towards an old threadbare broomstick which was leaning on the other side of the brambles. At the sight, the mop threw Charles into the nettles and went bouncing flirtatiously towards the broomstick too, looking just like a granny on an outing.

Charles and Nirupam picked themselves bad-temperedly up. They listened. The motorists on the road seemed to have got tired of sounding their horns. They looked. Beyond the jumping hoe and the nuzzling mop, there was a well-made campfire. Behind the fire, con-cealed by more brambles, was a small orange tent. Brian Wentworth was standing by the tent, glowering at them.

"I thought I'd got at least one of you arrested," Brian said. "Get lost, can't you! Or are you trying to get me caught?"

"No, we are not!" Charles said angrily. "We're – Hey, listen!"

Somewhere uphill, in the thick part of the wood, a dog gave one whirring, excited bark, and stopped suddenly. Birds were clapping up out of the trees. And Charles's straining ears could also hear a rhythmic swishing, as of heavy feet marching through undergrowth.

"That's the police," he said.

"You fools! You've brought them down on me!" Brian said in a screaming whisper. He grabbed the old broom from between the mop and the hoe and, in one practised jump, he was on the broom and gliding away across the brambles.

"*He* did the birds in Music," Nirupam said, and snatched the hoe. Charles seized the mop and both of them set off after Brian, wavering and hopping across the brambles and in among low trees. Charles kept his head down, because branches were raking at his hair, and thought that Nirupam must be right. Those birds had appeared promptly in time to save Brian having to sing. And a parrot shouting "Cuckoo!" was exactly Brian's kind of thing.

They were catching the broom up, not because they wanted to, but because the mop and the hoe were plainly determined to stay with the broom. They must have spent years together in the groundsman's hut and, Charles supposed irritably, they had got touchingly fond of one another. Nothing he or Nirupam could do would make either implement go a different way. Shortly, Brian was gliding among the trees only a few yards ahead of them.

He turned and glared at them. "Leave me alone! You've spoilt my escape and made me lose my tent. Go away!"

"It was the mop and the hoe," said Charles.

"The police are looking for you, not us," Nirupam panted. "What did you expect? You went missing."

"I didn't expect two great idiots crashing about the forest and bringing the police after me," Brian snarled. "Why couldn't you stay in school?"

"If you didn't want us, you shouldn't have written all that rubbish about a witch putting a spell on you," said

144

Charles. "There's an Inquisitor coming today because of you."

"Well, you advised me to do it," Brian said.

Charles opened his mouth and shut it again, quite unable to speak for indignation. They were coming to the edge of the woods now. He could see green fields through a mass of yellow hazel leaves, and he tried to turn the mop aside yet again. If they came out of the wood, they would be seen at once. But the mop obstinately followed the broom.

As they forced their way among whippy hazel boughs, Nirupam panted severely, "You ought to be glad of some friends with you, Brian."

Brian laughed hysterically. "Friends! I wouldn't be friends with either of you if you paid me! Everyone in 2Y laughs at you!"

As Brian said this, there was a sudden clamour of dog noises behind them in the wood. A voice shouted something about a tent. It was plain that the police had found Brian's camp. Brian and the broomstick put on speed and surged out into the field beyond. Charles and Nirupam found themselves being dragged anyhow through the hazel boughs as the mop and the hoe tried to keep up.

Scratched and breathless, they were whirled out into the field on the side of the wood that faced the town. Brian was some way ahead, flying low and fast downhill, towards a clump of trees in the middle of the field. The mop and the hoe surged after him.

"I know Brian is nasty, but I had always thought it was his situation before this," Nirupam remarked, in jerks, as the hoe kangaroo-hopped down the field.

Charles could not answer at once, because he was not sure that a person's character could be separated from their situation in quite this way. While he was wondering how you said this kind of thing aboard a speeding, wallowing mop, when you were hanging on with one hand and holding your glasses with the other, Brian reached the clump of trees and disappeared among them. They heard his voice again, shrill and annoyed, echoing out of the trees.

"Is Brian *trying* to bring the police after us?" Nirupam panted.

Both of them looked over their shoulders, expecting men and dogs to come charging out through the edge of the wood. There was nothing. Next moment, they were swishing through low branches covered with carroty beech leaves. The mop and the hoe jolted to a stop. Charles put his nettled legs down and stood up in a windy rustling space surrounded by pewter-coloured tree trunks. He stared at Estelle Green, looking as if she had mislaid a horse. He stared at Nan Pilgrim in ragged pink silk, with the broomstick hopping and sidling affectionately round her.

Brian was standing angrily beside them. "Look at this!" he said to Charles and Nirupam. "The place is alive with you lot! Why can't you let a person run away in peace?"

"Will one of you please shut Brian up," Estelle said, with great dignity. "We are just about to say a spell that will rescue us all."

"These trees are called the Portway Oaks," Nan explained, and bit the inside of her cheek in order not to laugh. Nirupam riding a hoe was one of the funniest things she had ever seen. And Charles Morgan's mop looked as if he had slain an old age pensioner. But she knew she and Estelle looked equally silly, and the boys had not laughed at them.

Brian was still talking angrily. Nirupam let the hoe loose to jump delightedly around the broom and clapped one long brown hand firmly over Brian's mouth. "Go ahead," he said.

"And make it quick," said Charles.

146

Nan and Estelle bent over their fluttering piece of paper again. The old lady had written just one strange word three times at the top of the paper. Under that, as she had told them, she had written, in shaky capitals, how to say this word: KREST-OH-MAN-SEE. After that she had put, *Go to Portway Oaks and say word three times*. The rest of the paper was full of a very wobbly map.

Estelle and Nan pronounced the word together, three times. "Chrestomanci, Chrestomanci, Chrestomanci."

"Is that all?" asked Nirupam. He took his hand from Brian's face.

"Somebody swindled you!" Brian said. "That's no spell!"

It seemcd as if a great gust of wind hit the clump of trees. The branches all round them lashed, and creaked with the strain, so that the air was full of the rushing of leaves. The dead orange leaves from the ground leapt in the air and swirled round them all, round and round, as if the inside of the clump was the centre of a whirlwind. This was followed by a sudden stillness. Leaves stayed where they were, in the air, surrounding everyone. No one could see anything but leaves, and there was not a sound to be heard from anywhere. Then, very slowly, sound began again. There was a gentle rustling as the suspended leaves dropped back to the ground. Where they had been, there was a man standing.

He seemed utterly bewildered. His first act was to put his hands up and smooth his hair, which was a thing that hardly needed doing, since the wind had not disturbed even the merest wisp of it. It was smooth and black and shiny as new tar. Having smoothed his hair, this man rearranged his starched white shirt cuffs and straightened his already straight pale grey cravat. After that, he carefully pulled down his dove-mauve waistcoat and, equally carefully, brushed some imaginary dust off his beautiful dove-grey suit. All the while he was doing this, he was looking from one to the other of the five of them in increasing perplexity. His eyebrows rose higher with everything he saw.

They were all thoroughly embarrassed. Nirupam tried to hide behind Charles as the man looked at his little blue shorts. Charles tried to slither behind Brian. Brian tried to knock the mud off the knees of his jeans without looking as if he was. The man's eyes turned to Nan. They were bright black eyes, which did not seem quite as bewildered as the rest of the man's face, and they made Nan feel that she would rather have had no clothes on at all than a ragged pink balldress. The man looked on towards Estelle, as if Nan were too painful a sight. Nan looked at Estelle too. Estelle, as she set her hard hat straight, was gazing adoringly up into the man's handsome face.

That was all we needed! Nan thought. Evidently this was the kind of man that Estelle fell instantly in love with. So, not only had they somehow summoned up an over-elegant stranger, but they were no nearer being safe and, to crown it all, there would probably be no sense to be had from Estelle from now on.

"Bless my soul!" murmured the man. He was now staring at the mop, the hoe and broom, which were jigging about in a little group like an old folks' reunion. "I think you'd *definitely* better go," he said to them. All three implements vanished, with a faint whistling sound. The man turned to Nan. "What are we all doing here?" he said, a little plaintively. "And where are we?"

Chapter Twelve

A dog barked excitedly up the hill. Everyone except the stranger jumped.

"I think we must go now, sir," Nirupam said politely. "That was a police dog. They were looking for Brian, but I think they're looking for the rest of us now."

"What do you expect them to do if they find you?" the man asked.

"Burn us," said Charles, and his thumb ran back and forth over the fat blister on his finger.

"We're all witches, you see, except Estelle," Nan explained.

"So if you don't mind us leaving you—" said Nirupam.

"How very barbarous," said the man. "I think it would be much better if the police and their dogs simply didn't see this clump of trees where we all are, don't you?" He looked vaguely round to see what they thought of this idea. Everyone looked dubious, and Brian downright scornful. "I assure you," the man said to Brian, "that if you go into the field outside and look, you will not see these trees any more than the police will. If the word of an enchanter is not enough for you, go out and see for yourself."

"What enchanter?" Brian said rudely. But of course no one dared leave the trees. They all waited, with their backs prickling, while the voices of policemen came slowly nearer. Finally, they seemed to be just outside the trees.

149

"Nothing," they heard a policeman saying. "Everyone go back and concentrate on the woods. Hills and MacIver, you two go down and see what those motorists by the hedge are waving about. The rest of you get the dogs back to that tent and start again from there."

After that, the voices all went away. Everyone relaxed a little, and Nan even began to hope that the stranger might be some help. But then he went all plaintive again. "Would one of you tell me where we are now?" he said.

"Just outside Larwood Forest," Nan said. "Hertfordshire."

"In England, the British Isles, the world, the solar system, the Milky Way, the Universe," Brian said scornfully.

"Ah yes," said the man. "But which one?" Brian stared. "I mean," the man said patiently, "do you happen to know *which* world, galaxy, universe etcetera? There happen to be infinite numbers of them, and unless I know which this one is, I shall not find it very easy to help you."

This gave Charles a very strange feeling. He thought of outer space and bug-eyed monsters and his stomach turned over. His eyes ran over the man's elegant jacket, fascinated, trying to make out if there was room under it for an extra pair of arms. There was not. The man was obviously a human being. "You're not really from another world, are you?" he said.

"I am precisely that," said the man. "Another world full of people just like you, running side by side with this one. There are myriads of them. So which one *is* this one?"

As far as most of them knew, the world was just the world. Everyone looked blank, except Estelle. Estelle said shyly, "There is *one* other world. It's the one the witches' rescue people send witches into to be safe."

"Ah!" The man turned to Estelle, and Estelle blushed

150

violently. "Tell me about this safe world."

Estelle shook her head. "I don't know any more," she whispered, overwhelmed.

"Then let's get at it another way," the man suggested. "You tell me all the events that led up to you summoning me here—"

"Is Chrestomanci your name then?" Estelle interrupted in an adoring whisper.

"I'm usually called that. Yes," said the man. "Was it you who summoned me then?"

Estelle nodded. "Some spell!" Brian said jeeringly.

Brian was plainly determined not to help in any way. He stayed scornfully silent while the rest of them explained the events which had led up to their being here. Nobody told Chrestomanci quite everything. Brian's contemptuous look made it all feel like a pack of lies anyway. Nan did not mention her meeting with Mr Wentworth on his hearthrug. She felt rather noble not saying anything about that, considering the way Brian was behaving. She did not mention the way she had described the food, either, though Charles did. On the other hand, Charles did not feel the need to mention the *Simon Says* spell. Nirupam told Chrestomanci about that, but he somehow forgot to say that Dan Smith had eaten Charles's shoes. And when the rest of them had finished, Chrestomanci looked at Brian.

"Your narrative now, please," he said politely.

It was a very powerful politeness. Everyone had thought that Brian was not going to tell anything at all, but, grudgingly, he did. First he admitted to causing the birds in Music. Then he claimed that Charles had advised him in the night to run away from school and confuse his trail by blaming the witch. And, while Charles was still stuttering with anger over that, Brian coolly explained that he had discovered Charles was a witch the next morning anyway and got Charles to take him to Matron so that Matron could see the effects of the

151

Evil Eye at first hand. Finally, more grudgingly still, he confessed that he had written the anonymous note to Mr Crossley and started everything. Then, as an afterthought, he turned on Nan.

"And you kept stealing my broomstick, didn't you?"

"It's not yours. It belongs to the school," said Nan.

At the same time, Charles was saying angrily to Chrestomanci, "It's not true I advised him to blame the witch!"

Chestomanci was staring vaguely up into the beech trees and did not seem to hear. "The situation is quite impossible," he remarked. "Let us all go and see the old lady who used to run the witches' rescue service."

This struck them all as an excellent idea. It was clear the old lady could rescue them if she wanted. They agreed vigorously. Nirupam said, "But the police—"

"Invisibly, of course," said Chrestomanci. He was still obviously thinking of something else. He turned to walk away between the tree trunks, and, as he did so, everyone flicked out of sight. All that could be seen was the rustling circle of autumn beeches. "Come along," said Chrestomanci's voice.

There followed a minute or so of almost indescribable confusion. It started with Nan assuming she had no body and walking into a tree. She was just as solid as ever, and knocked herself quite silly for a second. "Oh sorry!" she said to the tree. The rest of them somehow forced their way under the low branches and found themselves out in the field. There, the first thing everybody saw was two cars parked almost in the hedge below, and a number of people from the cars leaning over the hedge to talk to two policemen. From the way all the people kept pointing up at the wood, it was clear they were describing how they saw two witches ride across the road on a mop and a hoe. That panicked everyone. They all set off the other way, towards the town, in a hurry. But as soon as they did, they saw that there was no one ahead of them and waited for the rest to catch up. Then they heard someone speak some way ahead, and ran to catch up. But of course they could not tell where the people they were running after were. Shortly, nobody knew where anybody was or what to do about it.

"Perhaps," Chrestomanci's voice said out of the air, "you could all bring yourselves to hold hands? I have no idea where the Old Gate House is, you see."

Thankfully, everyone grabbed for everyone else. Nan found herself holding Brian's hand and Charles Morgan's. She had never thought the time would come when she would be glad to do that. Estelle had managed to be the one holding Chrestomanci's hand. That became clear when the line of them began to move briskly down to the path that led into town and Estelle's voice could be heard in front, piping up in answer to Chrestomanci's questions.

As soon as there was no chance of anyone else hearing them, Chrestomanci began asking a great many questions. He asked who was prime minister, and which were the most important countries, and what was the EEC, and how many world wars there had been. Then he asked about things from History. Before long, everyone was giving him answers, and feeling a little superior, because it was really remarkable the number of things Chrestomanci seemed not to know. He had heard of Hitler, though he asked Brian to refresh his memory about him, but he had only the haziest notion about Gandhi or Einstein, and he had never heard of Walt Disney or reggae. Nor had he heard of Dulcinea Wilkes. Nan explained about Dulcinea, and found herself saying, with great pride, that she was descended from Dulcinea.

Why am I saying that? she thought, in sudden alarm. I don't really know it's safe to tell him! And yet, as soon as she thought that, Nan began to see why she had said it. It was the way Chrestomanci was asking those questions. It reminded Nan of the time she had kept coming out in a rash, and her aunt had taken her to a very important specialist. The specialist had worn a very good suit, though it was nothing like as beautiful as Chrestomanci's, and he had asked questions in just the same way, trying to get at Nan's symptoms. Remembering this specialist made Nan feel a lot more hopeful. If you thought of Chrestomanci, in spite of his vagueness and his elegance, as a sort of specialist trying to solve their problems, then you could believe that he might just be able to help them. He was certainly a strong and expert witch. Perhaps he could make the old lady send them somewhere really safe.

When the path led them into the busy streets of the town, Chrestomanci stopped asking questions, but it was clear to Nan that he went on finding symptoms. He made everyone stop while he examined a lorry parked by the supermarket. It was just an ordinary lorry with Leyland on the front of it and Heinz Meanz Beanz on the side, but Chrestomanci murmured "Good Lord!" as if he was really astonished, before dragging them over to look through the windows of the supermarket. Then he towed them up and down in front of some cars. This part was really frightening. The car windows, the hubcaps, and the glass of the supermarket, all showed faint, misty reflections of the six of them. They were quite sure some of the people who were shopping would notice any second.

At last, Chrestomanci let Estelle drag him up the street as far as the tatty draper's where nobody ever seemed to buy anything. "How long have you had decimal currency?" he asked. While they were telling him, the misty reflection in the draper's window showed his tall shape bending to look at some packets of tights and a dingy blue nylon nightdress. "What are these stockings made of?"

154

"Nylon of course!" snapped Charles. He was wondering whether to let go of Nan's hand and run away.

Estelle, feeling much the same, heaved on Chrestomanci's hand and led them all in a rush to the doorway of the Old Gate House. She dragged them up the steps and hurriedly rang the bell before Chrestomanci could ask any more questions.

"There was no need to disturb her," Chrestomanci remarked. As he said it, the pointed porch dissolved away around them. Instead, they were in an old-fashioned drawing room, full of little tables with bobbly cloths on and ornaments on the cloth. The old lady was reaching for her stick and trying to lever herself out of her chair, muttering something about "An endless stream of callers today!"

Chrestomanci flicked into sight, tall and elegant and somehow very much in place in that old-fashioned room. Estelle, Nan, Charles, Nirupam and Brian also flicked into sight, and they looked as much out of place as people could be. The old lady sank back in her chair and stared.

"Forgive the intrusion, madam," Chrestomanci said.

The old lady beamed up at him. "What a splendid surprise!" she said. "No one's appeared like this for years! Forgive me if I don't get up. My knees are very arthritic these days. Would you care for some tea?"

"We won't trouble you, madam," said Chrestomanci. "We came because I understand you are a keeper of some kind of way through."

"Yes, I am," said the old lady. She looked dubious. "If you all have to use it, I suppose you have to, but it will take us hours. It's down in the cellar, you see, hidden from the Inquisitors under seven tons of coal."

"I assure you, we haven't come to ask you to heave coal, madam," said Chrestomanci. No, Charles thought, looking at Chrestomanci's white shirt cuffs. It will be us that does that. "What I really need to know,"

155

Chrestomanci went on, "is just which world it is on the other side of the way through."

"I haven't seen it," the old lady said regretfully. "But I've always understood that it's a world exactly like ours, only with no witchcraft."

"Thank you. I wonder—" said Chrestomanci. He seemed to have gone very vague again. "What do you know of Dulcinea Wilkes? Was there much witchcraft here before her day?"

"The Archwitch? Good gracious yes!" said the old lady. "There were witches all over the place long before Dulcinea. I think it was Oliver Cromwell who made the first laws against witches, but it may be before that. Somebody did once tell me that Elizabeth I was probably a witch. Because of the storm which wrecked the Spanish Armada, you know."

Nan watched Chrestomanci nodding as he listened to this and realized that he was collecting symptoms again. She sighed, and wondered whether to offer to start shovelling the coal.

Chrestomanci sighed a little too. "Pity," he said. "I was hoping the Archwitch was the key to the problems here. Perhaps Oliver Cromwell—?"

"I'm afraid I'm not a historian," the old lady said firmly. "And you won't find many people who know much more. Witch history is banned. All those kind of books were burnt long ago."

Charles, who was as impatient as Nan, butted in here. "Mr Wentworth knows a lot of witch history, but—"

"Yes!" Nan interrupted eagerly. "If you really want to know, you could summon Mr Wentworth here. He's a witch too, so it wouldn't matter." Here she realized that Brian was giving her a glare almost up to Charles Morgan's standards, and that Charles himself was staring at her wildly. "Yes he is," she said. "You know he is, Brian. I met him out flying on his hearthrug last night, and he thought I was you on your broomstick."

156

That explained everything, Charles thought. The night Mr Wentworth had vanished, he had gone out flying. The window had been wide open and, now he understood, Charles could remember distinctly the bald place in front of the gas-fire where the ragged hearthrug had been. And it explained that time in detention, too, when he had thought his glasses were broken. They *were* broken, and Mr Wentworth had restored them by witchcraft.

"Can't you keep your big mouth shut?" Brian said furiously to Nan. He pointed to Chrestomanci. "How do we know he's safe? For all *we* know, he could be the Devil that you summoned up!"

"Oh, you flatter me, Brian," Chrestomanci said.

The old lady looked shocked. "What an unpleasant thing to say," she said to Brian. "Hasn't anyone told you that the Devil, however he appears, is *never* a perfect gentleman? Quite unlike this Mr – er – Mr—?" She looked at Chrestomanci with her eyebrows politely raised.

"Chrestomanci, madam," he said. "Which reminds me. I wish you would tell me how you came to give Estelle and Nan my name."

The old lady laughed. "Was that what the spell was? I had no idea. It has been handed down in my family from my great-grandmother's time, with strict instructions that it's only to be used in an emergency. And those two poor girls were in such trouble – but I refuse to believe you can be that old, my dear sir."

Chrestomanci smiled. "No. Brian will be sorry to hear that the spell must have been meant to call one of my predecessors. Now. Shall we go? We must go to your school and consult Mr Wentworth, evidently."

They stared at him, even the old lady. Then, as it dawned on them that Chrestomanci was not going to let them go into the coal-cellar to safety, everyone broke out into protests. Brian, Charles and Nan said, "Oh no!

157

Please!" The old lady said, "Aren't you taking rather a risk?" at the same moment as Nirupam said, "But I told you there's an Inquisitor coming to school!" And Estelle added, "Couldn't we just all stay here quietly while *you* go and see Mr Wentworth?"

Chrestomanci looked from Estelle, to Nirupam, to Nan, and then at Brian and Charles. He seemed astounded, and not vague at all. The room seemed to go very quiet and sinister and unloving. "What's all this?" he said. It was so gentle that they all shivered. "I did understand you, did I? The five of you, between you, turn your school upside down. You cause what I am sure is a great deal of trouble to a great many teachers and policemen. You summon me a long way from some extremely important business, in a manner which makes it very difficult for me to get back. And now you all propose just to walk out and leave the mess you've made. Is that what you mean?"

"I didn't summon you," said Brian.

"It wasn't our fault," Charles said. "I didn't ask to be a witch."

Chrestomanci looked at him with faint, chilly surprise. "Didn't you?" The way he said it made Charles actually wonder, for a moment, if he had somehow chosen to be born a witch. "And so," said Chrestomanci, "you think your troubles give you a right to get this lady into much worse trouble with the Inquisitors? Is that what you all say?"

Nobody said anything.

"I think we shall be going now," Chrestomanci said, "if you would all hold one another's hands again, please." Wordlessly, they all held out hands and took hold. Chrestomanci took hold of Brian's, but, before he took hold of Estelle's in the other hand, he took the old lady's veined and knobby hand and kissed it. The old lady was delighted. She winked excitedly at Nan over Chrestomanci's smooth head. Nan did not even feel up

158

to smiling back. "Lead the way, Estelle," Chrestomanci said, straightening up and taking Estelle's hand. They found themselves invisible again. And, the same instant, they were outside in the street.

Estelle set off towards Larwood House. If it had been anybody else but Estelle in the lead, Charles thought, they might have thought of taking the line of them somewhere else — anywhere else — because Chrestomanci would not know. But Estelle led them straight to school, and everyone else shuffled after, too crushed and nervous to do anything else. Brian was the only one who protested. Whenever there were no people about, his voice could be heard saying that it wasn't *fair*. "What did you girls have to fetch him for?" he kept saying.

By the time they were through the school gates and shuffling up the drive, Brian gave up protesting. Estelle led them to the main door, the grand one, which was only used for parents or visitors like Lord Mulke. There were two police cars parked on the gravel beside it, but they were empty and there was no one about.

Here, in a sharp scuffling of gravel, Brian made a determined effort to run away. To judge by the sounds, and by the way Estelle came feeling her way along Nirupam and Nan, Chrestomanci was after Brian like a shot. Three thumps, and a scatter of small stones, and Chrestomanci suddenly reappeared, beside the nearest police car. He seemed to be on his own, but his right arm was stiffly bent and jerking a little, as the invisible Brian writhed on the end of it.

"I do advise you all to keep quite close to me," he said, as if nothing had happened. "You will only be invisible within ten yards of me."

"I can make myself invisible," Brian's voice said, from beside Chrestomanci's dove-grey elbow. "I'm a witch too."

"Quite probably," Chrestomanci agreed. "But I am not a witch, as it happens. I am an enchanter. And, among other differences, an enchanter is ten times as strong as a witch. Who is at the end of the line now? Charles. Charles, will you be good enough to walk up the steps to the door and ring the bell?"

Charles trudged forward, towing the others behind him, and rang the bell. There seemed nothing else to do.

The door was opened almost at once by the school secretary. Chrestomanci stood there, apparently alone, with his dove-grey suit quite unruffled and not a hair out of place, smiling pleasantly at the secretary. It was hard to believe that he had Brian gripped in one hand and Estelle clinging to the other, and three more people crowded uncomfortably around him. He bowed slightly.

"Name of Chant," he said. "I believe you were expecting me. I'm the Inquisitor."

Chapter Thirteen

The school secretary dissolved into dither. She gushed. It was just as well. Otherwise she might have heard five gasps out of the air round Chrestomanci.

"Oh *do* come in, Inquisitor," the secretary gushed. "Miss Cadwallader is expecting you. And I'm awfully sorry – we seem to have got your name wrong. We were told to expect a Mr Littleton."

"Quite right," Chrestomanci said blandly. "Littleton is the Regional Inquisitor. But Head Office decided the matter was too grave to be merely Regional. I'm the Divisional Inquisitor."

"Oh!" said the secretary, and seemed quite overawed. She ushered Chrestomanci in and through the tiled hall. Chrestomanci stepped after her, slow and stately, in a way that allowed plenty of time for everyone to squeeze round him into the hall and tiptoe beside him across the tiles. The secretary threw wide the door to Miss Cadwallader's study. "Mr Chant, Miss Cadwallader. The Divisional Inquisitor." Chrestomanci went into the study even more slowly, lugging Brian and pulling Estelle. Nan and Nirupam squeezed after, and Charles just got in too by jamming himself against the doorpost as the secretary backed reverently out. He did not want to be left outside the circle of invisiblity.

Miss Cadwallader sprang forward in a quite unusual flutter and shook hands with Chrestomanci. The rest of them heard Brian thump away sideways as Chrestomanci let go of him. "Oh good morning, Inquisitor!"

"Morning, morning," said Chrestomanci. He seemed to have gone vague again. He looked absently round the room while he was shaking hands. "Nice place you have here, Miss – er – Cudwollander."

This was true. Perhaps on the grounds that she had to persuade government officials and parents that Larwood House was a really good school, Miss Cadwallader had surrounded herself in luxury. Her carpet was like deep crimson grass. Her chairs were purple clouds of softness. She had marble statues on her mantelpiece and large gilt frames round her hundred or so pictures. She had a cocktail cabinet with a little refrigerator built into it and a coffee-maker on top. Her hi-fi and tape-deck took up most of one wall. Charles looked yearningly at her vast television with a crinoline doll on top. It seemed years since he had watched any telly. Nan gazed at the wall of bright new books. Most of them seemed to be mystery stories. She would have loved to have a closer look at them, but she did not dare let go of Nirupam or Charles in case she never found them again.

"I'm so glad you approve, Inquisitor," fluttered Miss Cadwallader. "My room is entirely at your disposal, if you wish to use it to interview children in. I take it that you will need to interview some of the children in 2Y?"

"All the children in 2Y," Chrestomanci said gravely, "and probably all their teachers too." Miss Cadwallader looked thoroughly dismayed by this. "I shall expect to interview everyone in the school before I'm through," Chrestomanci went on. "I shall stay here for as long as it takes – weeks if necessary – to get to the bottom of this matter."

By this time, Miss Cadwallader was distinctly pale. She clasped her hands nervously. "Are you sure it's *that* serious, Inquisitor? It *is* only a boy in the second year who disappeared in the night. His father happens to be one of our masters here, which is really why we're so concerned. I know you were told that the boy left a large

162

number of notes accusing a witch of abducting him, but the police have telephoned since to say they have found a camp in the forest with the boy's scent on it. Don't you think the whole thing could be cleared up quite easily and quickly?"

Chrestomanci gravely shook his head. "I have been kept abreast of the facts too, Miss – er – Kidwelly. The boy has still not turned up, has he? One can't be too careful in a case like this. I think someone in 2Y knows more about this than you think."

Up to now, everyone listening had been feeling more and more relieved. If Miss Cadwallader had known there were four other people missing besides Brian, she would surely have said so. But their feelings changed at what Miss Cadwallader said next.

"You must interview a girl called Theresa Mullett straight away, Inquisitor, and I think you will find that the matter will be cleared up at once. Theresa is one of our *good* girls. She came to me in break and told me that the witch is almost certainly a child called Dulcinea Pilgrim. Dulcinea is *not* one of our good girls, Inquisitor, I'm sorry to say. Some of her journal entries have been very free-spoken and disaffected. She questions everything and makes jokes about serious matters. If you like, I can send for Dulcinea's journal and you can see for yourself."

"I shall read all the journals in 2Y," said Chrestomanci, "in good time. But is this all you have to go on, Miss – er – Collander? I can't find a girl a witch simply on hearsay and a few jokes. It's not professional. Have you no other suspects? Teachers, for instance—"

"Teachers here are all above suspicion, Inquisitor." Miss Cadwallader said this very firmly, although her voice was a little shrill. "But 2Y as a class are not. It is a sad fact, Inquisitor, in a school like this, that a number of children come to us as witch-orphans, having had one or both parents burnt. There are an unusual number of

these in 2Y. I would pick out, for your immediate attention, Nirupam Singh, who had a brother burnt, Estelle
Green, whose mother is in prison for helping witches
escape, and a boy called Charles Morgan, who is almost
as undesirable as the Pilgrim girl."

"Dear me! What a poisonous state of affairs!" said
Chrestomanci. "I see I must get down to work at once."

"I shall leave you this room of mine to work in then,
Inquisitor," Miss Cadwallader said graciously. She
seemed to have recovered from her flutter.

"Oh, I can't possibly trouble you," Chrestomanci
said, quite as graciously. "Doesn't your Deputy Head
have a study I could use?"

Intense relief shone through Miss Cadwallader's
stately manner. "Yes, indeed he does, Inquisitor. What
an excellent idea! I shall take you to Mr Wentworth
myself, at once."

Miss Cadwallader swept out of her room, almost too
relieved to be stately. Chrestomanci located Brian as
easily as if he could see him, took his arm and swept off
after her. The other four were forced to tiptoe furiously
to keep up. None of them wanted to see Mr Wentworth.
In fact, after what Miss Cadwallader had just said, the
one thing they all longed to do was to sneak off and run
away again. But the instant they got more than ten yards
away from Chrestomanci, there they would be, in
riding-clothes, little blue shorts and pink balldress, for
Miss Cadwallader or anyone else they passed to see.
That was enough to keep them all tiptoeing hard, along
the corridors and up the stairs.

Miss Cadwallader rapped on the glass of Mr Wentworth's study. "Come!" said Mr Wentworth's voice.
Miss Cadwallader threw the door open and made
ushering motions to Chrestomanci. Chrestomanci
nodded vaguely and once more made a slow and
imposing entry, with a slight dragging noise as he pulled
the resisting Brian through the doorway. That gave the

164

other four plenty of time to slip inside past Miss Cadwallader.

"I'll leave you with Mr Wentworth for now, Inquisitor," Miss Cadwallader said, in the doorway. Mr Wentworth, at that, looked up from his timetables. When he saw Chrestomanci, his face went pale, and he stood up slowly, looking thoroughly harrowed. "Mr Wentworth," said Miss Cadwallader, "this is Mr Chant, who is the Divisional Inquisitor. Come to my study for sherry before lunch, both of you, please." Then obviously feeling she had done enough, Miss Cadwallader shut the door and went away.

"Good morning," Chrestomanci said politely.

"G – good morning," said Mr Wentworth. His hands were trembling and rustling the timetables. He swallowed, loudly. "I – I didn't realize there were Divisional Inquisitors. New post, is it?"

"Oh, do you not have Divisional ones?" Chrestomanci said. "What a shame. I thought it sounded so imposing."

He nodded. Everybody was suddenly visible again. Nan, Charles and Nirupam all tried to hide behind each other. Brian was revealed tugging crossly to get his arm loose from Chrestomanci, and Estelle was hanging on to Chrestomanci's other hand again. She let go hurriedly and took her hard hat off. But it was quite certain that Mr Wentworth did not notice any of these things. He backed against the window, staring from Chrestomanci to Brian, and he was more than harrowed now: he was terrified.

"What's going on?" he said. "Brian, what have you lent yourself to?"

"Nothing," Brian said irritably. "He isn't an Inquisitor. He's an enchanter or something. It's not my fault he's here."

"What does he want?" Mr Wentworth said wildly. "I haven't anything I can give him!"

"My dear sir," said Chrestomanci, "please try and be calm. I only want your help."

Mr Wentworth pressed back against the window. "I don't know what you mean!"

"Yes you do," Chrestomanci said pleasantly. "But let me explain. I am Chrestomanci. This is the title that goes with my post, and my job is controlling witchcraft. My world is somewhat more happily placed than yours, I believe, because witchcraft is not illegal there. In fact, this very morning I was chairing a meeting of the Walpurgis Committee, in the middle of making final arrangements for the Hallowe'en celebrations, when I was rather suddenly summoned away by these pupils of yours—"

"Is that why you're wearing those beautiful clothes?" Estelle asked admiringly.

Everyone winced a little, except for Chrestomanci, who seemed to think it was a perfectly reasonable question. "Well, no, to be quite honest," he said. "I like to be well dressed, because I am always liable to be called elsewhere, the way you called me. But I have to confess that I have several times been fetched away in my dressing-gown, in spite of all my care." He looked at Mr Wentworth again, obviously expecting him to have calmed down by now. "There are real problems with this particular call," he said. "Your world is all wrong, in a number of ways. That's why I would appreciate your help, sir."

Unfortunately, Mr Wentworth was by no means calm. "How dare you talk to me like this!" he said. "It's pure blackmail! You'll get no help from me!"

"Now that is unreasonable, sir," Chrestomanci said. "These children are in acute trouble. You are in the same trouble yourself. Your whole world is in even greater trouble. Please, try if you can, to forget that you have been scared for years, both for yourself and Brian, and listen to the questions I am going to ask you."

But Mr Wentworth seemed unable to be reasonable. Nan looked at him sorrowfully. She had always thought he was such a firm person up till now. She felt quite disillusioned. So did Charles. He remembered Mr Wentworth's hand on his shoulder, pushing him back into detention. He had thought that hand had been shaking with anger, but he realized now that it had been terror.

"It's a trick!" Mr Wentworth said. "You're trying to get a confession out of me. You're using Brian. You *are* an Inquisitor!"

Just as he said that, there was a little tap at the door, and Miss Hodge came brightly in. She had just given 2Y an English lesson — the last one until next Tuesday, thank goodness! Naturally, she had noticed that four other people besides Brian were now missing. At first, she had assumed that they were all being questioned by the Inquisitor. They were the obvious ones. But then someone in the staff room had remarked that the Inquisitor still hadn't come. Miss Hodge saw at once that this was the excuse she needed to go to Mr Wentworth and start sympathizing with him about Brian. She came in as soon as she had knocked, to make quite sure that Mr Wentworth did not get away again.

The room for an instant seemed quite full of people, and poor Mr Wentworth was looking so upset and shouting at what seemed to be the Inquisitor after all. The Inquisitor gave Miss Hodge a vague look and then waved his hand, just the smallest bit. After that, there did only seem to be the Inquisitor and Mr Wentworth in the room besides Miss Hodge. But Miss Hodge knew what she had seen. She thought about it while she said what she had come to say.

"Oh, Mr Wentworth, I'm afraid there are four more people missing from 2Y now." And the four people had all been here in the room, Miss Hodge knew. Wearing such peculiar things too. And Brian had been there as

167

well. That settled it. Mr Wentworth might look upset, but he was not sorrowing about Brian. That meant that she either had to think of some other way to get his attention, or use the advantage she knew she had. The man who was supposed to be an Inquisitor was politely putting forward a chair for her to sit in. A smooth villain. Miss Hodge ignored the chair. "I think I'm interrupting a witches' Sabbath," she said brightly.

The man with the chair raised his eyebrows as if he thought she was mad. A very smooth villain. Mr Wentworth said, in a strangled sort of way, "This is the Divisional Inquisitor, Miss Hodge."

Miss Hodge laughed, triumphantly. "Mr Wentworth! You and I both know that there's no such thing as a Divisional Inquisitor! Is this man annoying you? If so, I shall go straight to Miss Cadwallader. I think she has a right to know that your study is full of witches."

Chrestomanci sighed and wandered away to Mr Wentworth's desk, where he idly picked up one of the timetables. Mr Wentworth's eyes followed him as if Chrestomanci was annoying him very much, but he said, in a resigned way, "There's absolutely no point in going to Miss Cadwallader, Miss Hodge. Miss Cadwallader has known I'm a witch for years. She takes most of my salary in return for not telling anyone."

"I didn't know you—!" Miss Hodge began. She had not realized Mr Wentworth was a witch too. That made quite a difference. She smiled more triumphantly than before. "In that case, let me offer you an alliance against Miss Cadwallader, Mr Wentworth. You marry me, and we'll both fight her."

"Marry you?" Mr Wentworth stared at Miss Hodge in obvious horror. "Oh no. You can't. I can't—"

Brian's voice said out of the air, "I'm not having *her* as a mother!"

Chrestomanci looked up from the timetable. He shrugged. Brian appeared on the other side of the room,

168

looking as horrified as Mr Wentworth. Miss Hodge smiled again. "So I was right!" she said.

"Miss Hodge," Mr Wentworth said, shakily trying to sound calm and reasonable, "I'm sorry to disappoint you, but I can't marry anyone. My wife is still alive. She was arrested as a witch, but she managed to get away through someone's back-garden and get to the witches' rescue service. So you see—"

"Well, you'd better pretend she was burnt," Miss Hodge said. She was very angry. She felt cheated. She marched up to Mr Wentworth's desk and took hold of the receiver of Mr Wentworth's telephone. "You agree to marry me, or I ring the police about you. Now."

"No, please—!" said Mr Wentworth.

"I mean it," said Miss Hodge. She tried to pick the receiver up off the telephone. It seemed to be stuck. Miss Hodge jiggled it angrily. It gave out a lot of tinkling, but it would not seem to move. Miss Hodge looked round to find Chrestomanci looking at her in an interested way. "You stop that!" she said to him.

"When you tell me one thing," Chrestomanci said. "You don't seem at all alarmed to find yourself in a roomful of witches. Why not?"

"Of course I'm not," Miss Hodge retorted. "I pity witches. Now will you please allow me to ring the police about Mr Wentworth. He's bccn deceiving everyone for years!"

"But my dear young lady," said Chrestomanci, "so have you. The only sort of person who would behave as you do must be a witch herself."

Miss Hodge stared at him haughtily. "I have never used a spell in my life," she said.

"A slight exaggeration," Chrestomanci said. "You used one small spell, to make sure no one knew you were a witch."

Why didn't I think of that? Charles wondered, watching the look of fear and dismay grow in Miss

Hodge's face. He was very shaken. He could not get used to the idea that his second witch had probably been Brian's mother.

Miss Hodge once more jiggled the telephone. It was still stuck. "Very well," she said. "I'm not afraid of you. You can disable all the phones in the school if you like, but you won't stop me going and telling everyone I meet, about you and Mr Wentworth and Brian, and the other four, unless Mr Wentworth agrees to marry me this instant. I think I shall start with Harold Crossley." She made as if to turn away and leave the room. It was clear she meant it.

Chrestomanci sighed and put one finger down on the timetable he was holding, very carefully and precisely, in the middle of one of the rectangles marked *Miss Hodge 2Y*. And Miss Hodge was not there any more. The telephone gave out a small ting, and she was gone. At the same moment, Nan, Estelle, Nirupam and Charles all found themselves visible again. It was clear to them that Miss Hodge was not just invisible in their place. The room felt empty of her, and a small gust of wind ruffling the papers on Mr Wentworth's desk seemed to prove she was gone.

"Fancy her being a witch!" said Nirupam. "Where is she?"

Chrestomanci examined the timetable. "Er – next Tuesday, I believe. That should give us time to sort out this wretched situation. Unless we are very unlucky, of course." He looked at Mr Wentworth. "Perhaps you would be ready to help us do that now, sir?"

But Mr Wentworth sank into the chair behind his desk and covered his face with his hands.

"You never told me Mum got away," Brian said to him accusingly. "And you never said a word about Miss Cadwallader."

"You never told me you intended to go and camp in the forest," Mr Wentworth said wearily. "Oh Lord!

170

Where shall I get an extra teacher from? I've got to find someone to take Miss Hodge's lessons this afternoon somehow."

Chrestomanci sat in the chair he had put out for Miss Hodge. "It never ceases to amaze me," he said, "the way people always manage to worry about the wrong things. My dear sir, do you realize that you, your son, and four of your pupils, are all likely to be burnt unless we do something? And here are you worrying about time-tables."

Mr Wentworth lifted his harrowed face and stared past Chrestomanci. "How did she *do* it?" he said. "How does she keep it up? How *can* Miss Hodge be a teacher and not use witchcraft at all? I use it all the time. How else can I have eyes in the back of my head?"

"One of the great mysteries of our time," Chrestomanci agreed. "Now please listen to me. You are aware, I believe, that there is at least one other world besides this one. It seems to be your custom to send escaped witches there. I presume your wife is there. What you may not realize is that these are only two out of a multitude of worlds, all very different from one another. I come from one of the other ones myself."

To everyone's relief, Mr Wentworth listened to this. "Alternative worlds, you mean?" he said. "There's been some speculation about that. If-worlds, counterfactuals, and so on. You mean they're real?"

"As real as you are," Chrestomanci said.

Nirupam was very interested in this. He doubled himself up on the floor beside Chrestomanci's beautifully creased trousers and said, "They are made from the great events in History, I believe, sir, where it is possible for things to go two ways. It is easiest to understand with battles. Both sides cannot win a battle, so each war makes two possible worlds, with a different side winning. Like the Battle of Waterloo. In our world, Napoleon lost it, but another world at once split off

171

from ours, in which Napoleon won the battle."

"Exactly," said Chrestomanci. "I find that world a rather trying one. Everyone speaks French there and winces at my accent. The only place they speak English there, oddly enough, is in India, where they are very British and eat treacle pudding after their curry."

"I should like that," Nirupam said.

"Everyone to his taste," Chrestomanci said with a slight shudder. "But, as you will see, exactly who won the Battle of Waterloo made a great deal of difference between those two worlds. And that is the rule. A surprisingly small change always alters the new world almost out of recognition. Except in the case of this world of yours, where we all now are." He looked at Mr Wentworth. "This is what I need your help about, sir. There is something badly wrong with this world. The fact that witches are extremely common, and illegal, should have made as much difference here as it does in my own world, where witches are equally common, but quite legal. But it does not. Estelle, perhaps you can tell us about the world where the witches' rescue service sends witches."

Estelle beamed up at him adoringly from where she was sitting crosslegged on the floor. "The old lady said it was just like this one, only with no witchcraft," she said.

"And that is just the trouble," said Chrestomanci. "I know that world rather well, because I have a young ward who used to belong in it. And since I have been here, I have discovered that events in History here, cars, advertisements, goods in shops, money — everything I can check — are all exactly the same as those in my ward's world. And this is quite wrong. No two worlds are ever this alike."

Mr Wentworth was attending quite keenly now. He frowned. "What do you think has gone wrong?" And Nan thought, So he *was* finding out symptoms!

Chrestomanci looked round them all, vaguely and

dubiously, before he said, "If you'll forgive me saying, your world should not exist." They all stared. "I mean it," Chrestomanci said, apologetically. "I have often wondered why there is so little witchcraft in my ward's world. I see now that it is all in this one. Something – I don't know what – has caused your world to separate from the other one, taking all the witchcraft with it. But instead of breaking off cleanly, it has somehow remained partly joined to the first world, so that it almost *is* that world. I think there has been some kind of accident. You shouldn't get a civilized world where witches are burnt. As I said, it ought not to exist. So, as I have been trying to explain to you all along, Mr Wentworth, I urgently need a short history of witchcraft, in order to discover what kind of accident happened here. Was Elizabeth I a witch?"

Mr Wentworth shook his head. "Nobody knows for sure. But witchcraft didn't seem to be that much of a problem in her reign. Witches were mostly just old women in villages then. No – modern witchcraft really started soon after Elizabeth I died. There seems to have been a big increase in about 1606, when the first official bone-fires started. The first Witchcraft Edict was passed in 1612. Oliver Cromwell passed more. There had been thirty-four Witchcraft Acts passed by 1760, the year Dulcinea Wilkes—"

But Chrestomanci held up one hand to stop him there. "Thank you. I know about the Archwitch. You've told me what I need to know. The present state of witchcraft began quite suddenly soon after 1600. That means that the accident we're looking for must have happened around then. Have you any idea what it might be?"

Mr Wentworth shook his head again, rather glumly. "I haven't a notion. But – suppose you did know, what could you do about it?"

"One of two things," said Chrestomanci. "Either we could break this world away completely from the other

173

one, which I don't consider a good idea, because then you would certainly all be burnt—" Everybody shuddered, and Charles's thumb found itself running back and forth over the blister on his finger. "Or," said Chrestomanci, "and this is a much better idea, we could put your world back into the other one, where it really belongs."

"What would happen to us if you did?" asked Charles.

"Nothing much. You would simply melt quietly into the people you really are in that world," said Chrestomanci.

Everyone considered this in silence for a moment. "Can that really be done?" Mr Wentworth asked hopefully.

"Well," said Chrestomanci, "it can, as long as we can find what caused the split in the first place. It will take strong magic. But it *is* Hallowe'en and there ought to be a great deal of magic loose in this world particularly, and we can draw on that. Yes. I'm sure it can be done, though it may not be easy."

"Then let's do it," said Mr Wentworth. The idea seemed to restore him to his usual self. He stood up, and his eyes roved grimly across the riding clothes, the sky-blue shorts and Brian's jeans, and rested incredulously upon the tattered pink balldress. "If you lot think you can appear in class like that," he said. He was back to being a schoolmaster again.

"Er, leave Brian, I think," Chrestomanci said quickly.

"You will have plenty of time to reconsider in detention," Mr Wentworth finished. Nan, Estelle, Charles and Nirupam all scrambled hurriedly to their feet. And as soon as they were standing up, they found they were wearing school uniform. They looked round for Brian, but he did not seem to be there.

"I'm invisible again!" Brian said disgustedly, out of the air.

Chrestomanci was smiling. "Not bad, sir," he said to Mr Wentworth. Mr Wentworth looked pleased, and, as he shephered the four of them to the door, he smiled back at Chrestomanci in quite a friendly way.

"Why is Brian allowed to stay invisible?" Estelle complained, as Mr Wentworth marched them back towards the classroom.

"Because he gives Chrestomanci an excuse to go on staying here as an Inquisitor," Nirupam whispered. "He is supposed to be finding what the witch has done with Brian."

"But don't tell Brian," Charles muttered, as they arrived outside the door of 2Y. "He'd spoil it. He's like that." The truth was, he was not so sure he would not spoil things himself if he got the chance. Nothing had been changed. He was still in as much trouble as ever.

Chapter Fourteen

Mr Wentworth opened the door and ushered the four of them into the classroom, into a blast of stares and whispers. "I'm afraid I had to kidnap these four," Mr Wentworth said to Mr Crossley, who happened to be teaching the rest. "We've been arranging my study for the Inquisitor to use."

Mr Crossley seemed to believe this without question. 2Y, to judge from their faces, felt it was an awful let-down. They had expected all four of them to have been arrested. But they made the best of it.

"Mr Towers is looking for you two," Simon whispered righteously to Nirupam and Charles. And Theresa said to Estelle, "Miss Phillips wants you." Nan was lucky. Miss Phillips never remembered Nan if she could help it.

They had arrived back so late that there was only a short piece of lesson left before lunch time. When the bell rang for lunch, Charles and Nirupam kept to the thickest crowds. Neither of them wanted Mr Towers to see them. But Charles had his usual bad luck. Mr Towers was on duty at the door of the dining hall. Charles was very relieved when he slipped past without Mr Towers showing any interest in him at all.

Nirupam nudged Charles as they sat down after grace. Chrestomanci was sitting beside Miss Cadwallader at high table, looking bland and vague. Everyone craned to look at him. Word went round that this was the Divisional Inquisitor.

"I don't fancy getting on the wrong side of him," Dan Smith observed. "You can see that sleepy look's just there to fool you."

"He looks feeble," said Simon. "I'm not going to let him scare me."

Charles craned to look too. He knew what Simon meant, but he was quite sure by now that Chrestomanci's vague look was as deceptive as Dan thought. Mr Wentworth was up at high table too. Charles wondered where Brian was and how Brian would get any lunch.

Charles turned back to the table to hear Theresa saying, "He's so super looking, he makes me feel quite weak!"

To everyone's surprise, Estelle jumped to her feet and leant across the table, glaring at Theresa. "Theresa Mullet!" she said. "You just dare be in love with the Inquisitor and see what you get! He's mine. I met him first and *I* love him! So you just dare!"

Nobody said a word for a moment. Theresa was too astonished even to giggle. Everyone was so unused to seeing Estelle so fierce that even the prefect in charge could not think what to say.

During the silence, it became clear how Brian was going to get lunch. Charles and Nirupam felt themselves being pushed apart by an invisible body. Both of them were jabbed by invisible elbows as the body climbed on to the bench between them and sat. "You'll have to let me eat off your plates," whispered Brian's voice. "I hope it's not stew."

Luckily, Simon broke the silence just as Brian spoke. He said, in a jeering, not-quite-believing way, "And what took you all so long to arrange for Mr Feeble Inquisitor?"

Ftom the way everyone looked then, Nan knew nobody had believed Mr Wentworth's excuse for an instant. She could see most of them suspected something like the truth. Help! thought Nan. "Well we had to put a lot of electric wiring into the study," she invented hastily. "He has to have a bright light arranged to shine into people's faces. It helps break them down."

"Not for electric shocks at all?" Dan asked hopefully.

"Some of it *may* have been," Nan admitted. "There were quite a lot of bare wires, and a sort of helmet-thing with electrodes sticking out of it. Charles wired that. Charles is very good with electricity."

"And what else?" Dan asked breathlessly. He was far too fascinated by now to notice he was talking to a girl.

"The walls were all draped in black," invented Nan. "Estelle and I did that."

Lunch was served just them. It was potato pie. This was fortunate for Brian, who dared not use a knife and fork, but not so lucky for Charles and Nirupam. Both of them gave grunts of indignation as a large curved chunk vanished from their plates. Brian had taken a handful from each. They were more annoyed still, when lumps of potato began to flop down between them.

"Don't waste it!"snapped Nirupam.

"Can't you tell where your mouth is?" Charles whispered angrily.

"Yes. But I don't know where my hands are," Brian whispered back. "*You* try, if you think you're so clever!"

While they whispered, Nan was being eagerly questioned by Dan, and forced to invent more and more Inquisitor's equipment for Mr Wentworth's study. "Yes, there *were* these things with little chromium screws in," she was saying. "I think you're right – those must have been thumbscrews. But some of them looked big enough to get an arm or a leg in. I don't think he stops at thumbs."

Nirupam dug Brian's invisible side with his elbow. "Attend to this!" he whispered. "It all has to be there if he calls Dan in."

"I'm not a fool," Brian's voice retorted with its mouth full.

"And of course there were a lot of other things we had to hang on the wall. All sizes of handcuffs," Nan went on. She was inspired now and her invention seemed boundless. She just could not seem to stop. Charles began to wonder if one small study could possibly hold all the things she was describing – or even only the half of it that Brian managed to remember.

Fortunately, Estelle, who was far too busy watching Chrestomanci to eat, caused a sudden diversion by shouting out, "Look, look! Miss Cadwallader's only using a fork, and *he's* using a knife and a fork! Oh, isn't he *brave*!"

At that, Nirupam seized the opportunity to try and shut Nan up. He gave her a sinister stare and said loudly, "You realize that the Inquisitor will probably be questioning every one of us very searchingly indeed, after lunch is over."

Though Nirupam meant this simply as a warning to Nan, it caused a worried silence. A surprising number of people did not seem very keen on the treacle tart which followed the potato pie. Nirupam seized that opportunity too. He took third and fourth helpings and shared them with Brian.

Straight after lunch, Mr Wentworth came and marshalled the whole of 2Y into alphabetical order. The worried silence became a scared one. From the looks they saw on the faces of the rest of the school, the scare was catching. Even seniors looked alarmed as 2Y were marched away. They marched upstairs and were lined up half in the passage and half on the stairs, while Mr Wentworth went into his study to tell Chrestomanci they were ready. Those at the front of the line were able to see that the wavy glass in the door was now black as night.

Then it turned out that Chrestomanci wanted to see them in reverse alphabetical order. They all had to march up and down and round again, so that Heather

Young and Ronald West were at the front of the line instead of Geoffrey Baines and Deborah Clifton. They did it with none of the usual grumbling and scuffling. Even Charles, who was quite certain that they were only marching to give Chrestomanci time to put all Nan's inventions in, found himself a little quiet and queasy, with his thumb rubbing at that blister. Heather and Ronald looked quite ill with terror. Dan Smith – who was third now that Brian was missing – asked Nirupam in an urgent whisper, "What's he going to do with us?"

Nirupam had no more idea than Dan. He had not even known that Chrestomanci really was going to question them. He tried to look sinister. "You'll see." Dan's face went cream-coloured.

Chrestomanci did not see people for the same length of time. Heather disappeared into the study for what seemed an endless age, and she came out as frightened as she went in. Ronald was only in for a minute, and he came out from behind the darkened door looking relieved. He leant across Dan and Nirupam to whisper to Simon, "No problem at all!"

"I knew there wouldn't be," Simon lied loftily.

"Quiet!" bellowed Mr Wentworth. "Next – Daniel Smith."

Dan Smith was not gone long either, but he did not come out looking as if there were no problem. His face was more like cheese than cream.

Nirupam was gone for much longer than either Nan or Charles had expected. When he came out, he was frowning and uneasy. He was followed by Simon. There was another endless wait. During it, the bell rang for afternoon lessons, and was followed by the usual surge of hurrying feet. The silence of lessons which came after that had gone on for so long before Simon came out that there was not a soul in 2Y who did not feel like an outcast. Simon came out at last. He was an odd colour. He would not speak to any of the friends who were leaning out of the line wanting to know what had happened. He just walked to the wall like a sleepwalker and leant against it, staring into space.

This did not make anyone feel better. Nan wondered what Chrestomanci was doing to people in there. By the time the three girls who came between her and Simon had all come out looking as bad as Heather Young, Nan was so scared that she could hardly make her legs work. But it was her turn. She had to go. She shuffled round the dark door somehow.

Inside, she stood and stared. Chrestomanci had indeed been very busy while 2Y marched up and down outside. Mr Wentworth's study was entirely lined with black curtains. A black carpet Nan had forgotten to invent covered the parquet floor. Hung on the walls and glimmering against the black background were manacles, a noose, festoons of chains, several kinds of scourge and a cat o' nine tails. There was a large can in one corner labelled *PETROL, DIV. INQ. OFFICE, FOR USE IN TORTURE ONLY.*

Chrestomanci himself was only dimly visible behind a huge glittering lamp, which reminded Nan uncomfortably of the light over an operating table. The light from it beamed on to Mr Wentworth's desk, draped in more black cloth, where there was a sort of jeweller's display of shiny thumbscrews and other displeasing ojects. The wired-up helmet was there. So was a bouquet of bare wires, spitting blue sparks. Behind those were a pile of fat black books.

"Can you see anything Brian forgot?" asked the dim shape of Chrestomanci.

Nan began to laugh. "I didn't say the carpet or the petrol!"

"Brian suggested a carpet. And I thought that corner looked a little bare," Chrestomanci admitted.

Nan pointed to the pile of black books. "What are those?"

"Disguised timetables," said Chrestomanci. "Oh – I see what you mean. Obviously they are Acts of Parliament and Witchcraft Edicts, torture manuals, and *The Observer's Guide to Witch-Spotting*. No Inquisitor would be without them."

Nan could tell from his voice that he was laughing. "I accuse you of enjoying yourself," she said, "while everyone outside gibbers."

"I confess to that." Chrestomanci came round the desk under the light. He pushed the spitting bunch of wires casually aside – it did not appear to give him any kind of shock – and sat on the black-draped desk so that his face was level with Nan's. She suddenly found it almost impossible to look away. "I accuse you of enjoying yourself too," he said.

"Yes I have!" Nan said defiantly. "For about the first time since I came to this beastly school!"

Chrestomanci looked at her almost anxiously. "You enjoy being a witch?"' Nan nodded vigorously. "And you've enjoyed making things up and describing them – thumbscrews and so on?" Nan nodded again. "Which did you enjoy most?" Chrestomanci asked.

"Oh, being a witch," Nan declared. "It's made me feel – well – just so confident, I suppose."

"Describe the things you've invented so far to do as a witch," said Chrestomanci.

"I —" Nan looked at Chrestomanci, lit from one side by the strong light of the lamp and, from the other, by the flickering wires, and was rather puzzled to find how little she had done as a witch. All she had done, when you came down to it, was to ride a broomstick and to give herself and Estelle the wrong kind of clothes and some decidedly odd collecting tins. "I haven't had much time to do things yet," she said.

"But Charles Morgan has had about the same amount of time, and according to the things people have been telling me, he has been very inventive indeed," Chrestomanci said. "Wouldn't you say that, now you've been a witch, and got your confidence, you might really prefer describing things even to witchcraft?"

Nan thought about it. "I suppose I would," she said, rather surprised. "If only we didn't have to do it in our journals!"

"Good," said Chrestomanci. "I think I can promise you one really good opportunity to describe things, nothing to do with journals. I told you it would take strong magic to put this world back into the one where it belongs. When I find the way to do it, I shall need everyone's help, in order to harness all the magic there is in the world to make the change. When the time comes, can I rely on you to explain all this?"

Nan nodded. She felt hugely flattered and responsible.

While she was feeling this way, Chrestomanci added, "Just as well you prefer describing things. I'm afraid you won't be a witch when the change comes." Nan stared at him. He was not joking. "I know you are descended from the Archwitch," Chrestomanci said, "but talents don't always descend in the same shape. Yours seem to have come to you in the form of making-up and describing. My advice is to stick with that if you can. Now name me one character out of History."

Nan blinked at the change of subject "Er – Christopher Columbus," she said miserably.

Chrestomanci took out a little gold notebook and unclipped a gold pencil. "Would you mind explaining who he was?" he said, a little helplessly.

It was astonishing the way Chrestomanci seemed not to know the most obvious things, Nan thought. She told him all about Christopher Columbus, as kindly as she could, and Chrestomanci wrote it down in his gold notebook. "Admirable," he murmured as he wrote. "Clear and vivid." The result was that Nan went out of the study one half delighted that Chrestomanci thought she was so good at describing things, and the other half desperately sad at not being a witch before long. Dan Smith's friend Lance Osgood, who was next one in, looked hard at Nan's face as she came out and did not know what to make of it.

Lance was not in the study long. Nor was Theresa Mullet, who came next. By this time, Estelle had just got up to the top of the stairs, near the end of the line. Estelle craned round the corner as Theresa came out, searching for signs of love in Theresa, but Theresa looked peevish and puzzled. Everyone saw that the Inquisitor had not treated Theresa with proper respect. Delia was whispering across to Heather about it when Charles went in.

Charles was not in the least frightened by this time. He was sure by now that Chrestomanci was treating everybody exactly as they deserved. He grinned when he saw the study all draped in black, and pushed his glasses up his nose to look at the things hung on the walls.

Chrestomanci was a dim shape behind the lamp and the spitting wires. "You approve?" he said.

"It's not bad," said Charles. "Where's Brian?"

"Over here," said Brian's voice. Two pairs of handcuffs on the black-draped wall lifted and jingled. "How long is this going on? I'm magicking bored already, and you've only got to M."

"Why have you got him in here?' Charles asked Chrestomanci. He kept his finger on his glasses in order to give Brian his best double-barrelled glare.

"I have my reasons," Chrestomanci said quietly. Quiet though it was, it made Charles feel as if something very cold and rather deadly was crawling down his back. "I want to talk to you," Chrestomanci continued, in the same quiet way, "about your *Simon Says* spell."

The cold spread from Charles's spine right through the rest of him, and settled particularly in his stomach. He knew that this interview was not going to be anything like the joke he had thought it would be. "What about it?" he muttered.

184

"I can't understand," Chrestomanci said, mild and puzzled and more deadly quiet than ever, "how you forgot to mention that spell. How did it come to slip your mind?"

It was like being embedded in ice. Charles tried to break out of the ice by blustering. "There was no point in telling you. It was only a spell – it wasn't important and Simon deserved it! And Nirupam took it off him anyway!"

"I beg your pardon. I wasn't aware that you had a defence," Chrestomanci said.

Sarcasm like this is hard enough to bear, and even worse if you know someone like Brian is listening in. Charles mustered another glare. But he found it hard to direct at Chrestomanci, hidden beyond the light, and swung it round at Brian again instead. Or rather, at the handcuffs where Brian might be. "It wasn't that important," he said.

Chrestomanci seemed more puzzled than ever. "Not important? My dear boy, what is so unimportant about a spell that could break the world up? You may know better, of course, but my impression is that Simon could easily have chanced to say something very silly, like – say – 'Two and two are five'. If he had, everything to do with numbers would have fallen apart at once. And since everything can be counted, everything would have come apart – the earth, the sun in the sky, the cells in bodies, anything else you can think of. No doubt you have a mind above such things, but I can't help finding that quite important myself."

Charles glowered at the handcuffs to disguise how awful this made him feel. And Brian had heard every word! "I didn't realize – how could I? Simon had it coming to him, anyway. He deserved something." He was rather glad, as he said it, that no one knew he intended to do something to Dan Smith next.

"Simon deserved it?" wondered Chrestomanci.

"Simon certainly has a large opinion of himself, but – Brian, you tell us. You have an ego at least as big as Simon's. Do you or Simon deserve to have such power put in your hands?"

"No," Brian's voice said sulkily. "Not to destroy the world."

Charles was cold all through with horror at what he had almost done. But he was not going to admit it. "Nirupam took it off him," he said, "before Simon did anything really."

"Brian seems to be learning," Chrestomanci remarked, "even if you are not, Charles. I grant you that, because magic is forbidden here, nobody has ever taught you what it can do or how to use it. But you could have worked it out. And you are still not thinking. Nirupam did *not* take that spell off Simon. He simply turned it back to front. *Nothing* the poor boy says comes true now. I have had to order him to keep his mouth shut."

"Poor boy!" Charles exclaimed. "You can't be sorry for him!"

"I am," said Brian's voice. "And if I hadn't been in the sick bay, I'd have tried to take it off him myself. I'd have managed better than Nirupam, too!"

"Now there, Charles," said Chrestomanci, "you have an excellent, example quite apart from rights and wrongs, of why it is such a bad idea to do things to people. Everyone is now sorry for Simon. Which is not what you want at all, is it?"

"No." Charles looked down at the shadowy black carpet and decided regretfully to think again about Dan Smith. This time he would get it right.

"Make him take the spell off Simon," Brian suggested.

"I doubt if he could," said Chrestomanci. "It's a fearsomely strong thing. Charles must have powers way up in the enchanter class in order to have worked it at all." Charles kept his face turned to the carpet, hoping that would hide the huge smug grin he could feel spreading on his face. "It will take a number of special circumstances to get that spell off Simon," Chrestomanci continued. "For a start, Charles must want to take the spell off. And he doesn't. Do you, Charles?"

"No," said Charles. The idea of Simon having to hold his tongue for the rest of his life gave him such pleasure that he did not bother to listen to all the names Brian began calling him. He held his finger out, into the lamplight, and admired the way the strong light and the spitting wires made patterns in the yellow cushion of blister. Wickedness was branded into him, he thought.

Chrestomanci waited for Brian to run out of names to call Charles. Then he said, "I'm sorry you feel this way, Charles. We are all going to need your help when we try to put this world back where it belongs. Won't you reconsider?"

"Not after the way you went on at me in front of Brian," said Charles. And he went on admiring his blister.

Chrestomanci sighed. "You and Brian are both as bad as one another," he said. "People in Larwood House are always developing into witches, Mr Wentworth tells me, but he tells me he has had no trouble in stopping any of them giving themselves away, until it came to you and Brian. Brian was so anxious to be noticed that he didn't care if he was burnt —"

"Hey!" Brian said indignantly.

So Chrestomanci was trying to make it fair by getting at Brian now, Charles thought. It was a bit late for that. He was not going to help.

"So he is going to have to help, or stay invisible for the rest of his life," Chrestomanci went on. He ignored indignant, miserable noises from Brian and turned to Charles. "You, Charles, seem to have bottled yourself up, hating everything, until your witchcraft came along and blew the stopper off you. Now, either you are going to have to bottle yourself up again or be burnt, *or* you

187

are going to have to help us. Since your talent for witch-craft is so strong, it seems certain that, in your right world, you will have an equally strong talent for something else, and you should find that easier. So which do you choose?"

Lose his witchcraft? Charles pressed one finger to his glasses and glared through the strong light at Chrestomanci. He did not think he even hated Simon or Dan as much as he hated Chrestomanci. "I'm going to go on being a witch! So there!"

The dim shape of Chrestomanci shrugged behind the light. "Warlock is the usual term for people who mess about the way you do. Very well. Now name me one historical personage, please."

"Jack the Ripper," snarled Charles.

The gold notebook flashed in the lamplight. "Thank you," said Chrestomanci. "Send the next person in as you go out."

As Charles turned and trudged to the door, Brian began calling him names again.

"Brian," Chrestomanci said quietly, "I told you I would take your voice away, and I shall if you speak to anyone else."

Typical! Charles thought angrily. He tore open the door, wondering what he dared do to Nan and Estelle for calling Chrestomanci here, and found himself staring into Delia Martin's face. He must have looked quite frightening. Delia went white. She actually spoke to him. "What's he like?"

"Magicking horrible!" Charles said loudly. He hoped Chrestomanci heard him.

Chapter Fifteen

The rest of 2Y shuffled slowly in and out of the study. Some came out white, some came out relieved. Estelle came out misty-eyed and beaming.

"Really!" said Theresa. "Some people!"

Estelle shot her a look of utter scorn and went up to Nan. She put both hands round one of Nan's ears and whispered wetly, "He says that where we're going, my mum won't be in prison!"

"Oh good!" said Nan, and she thought, in sudden excitement, And *my* mum will still be alive then!

Chrestomanci himself came out of the study with Geoffrey Baines, who was last, and exchanged a deep look with Mr Wentworth. Nan could tell that he had not found out how to change the world. She saw they were both worried.

"Right. In line and back to the classroom," shouted Mr Wentworth. He was looking so harrowed and hurried them down the stairs so fast that Nan knew Chrestomanci's luck was running out. Perhaps the real Inquisitor had arrived by now. The bell for the end of the first lesson rang as 2Y marched through the corridors, which increased the urgent feeling. Other classes hurried past them, and gave them looks of pitying curiosity.

Simon's friends kept trying to talk to him as they went. Simon shook his head madly and pointed to his mouth. "He knows who the witch is, but his lips are sealed," Ronald West said wisely.

This caused Delia and Karen to skip out of line and

walk beside Simon. "Tell us who the witch is, Simon," they whispered. "We won't say." The more Simon shook his head, the more they asked.

"Quiet!" barked Mr Wentworth.

Everyone filed into the classroom. There stood Mr Crossley, expecting to sit with 2Y while they wrote their journals.

"You'd better treat this as a free period, Harold," Mr Wentworth said to him. Mr Crossley nodded, highly pleased, and went off to the staff room, hoping to catch Miss Hodge there.

"Poor Teddy," Estelle whispered to Nan. "He doesn't know she's in next Tuesday. Mind you, I don't think she'd ever have him anyway."

Chrestomanci came into the classroom, looking suave and vague. No one could have guessed from the look of him that time was running out and he was probably just as anxious as Mr Wentworth. He coughed for attention. He got instant silence, complete and attentive. Mr Wentworth looked a little envious.

"This is a miserable affair," Chrestomanci said. "We have a witch in our midst. And this witch has cast a spell on Simon Silverson —"

The room rustled with people turning to look at Simon. Charles glowered. Simon was looking almost happy again. He was in the limelight, where he belonged.

"Now, most unfortunately," Chrestomanci went on, "someone made a well-meant but misguided effort to break the spell and turned it back to front." Nirupam looked morbid. "You can't blame this person," said Chrestomanci, "but the result is most unhappy. It was a very strong spell. Everything Simon now says does not only *not* happen, but it never *has* happened. I have had to warn Simon not to open his mouth until we get to the bottom of the matter."

As he said this, Chrestomanci's eyes turned, vaguely

190

and absently, towards Charles. Charles gave his blankest and nastiest look in reply. If Chrestomanci thought he could make him take the spell off this way, Chrestomanci could just think again. What Charles did not notice was that Chrestomanci's eyes moved towards Nan after that. Nobody else noticed at all, because three people had put their hands up: Delia, Karen and Theresa. Delia spoke for all three.

"Mr Inquisitor, sir, we told you who the witch is. It's Nan Pilgrim."

Estelle's desk went over with a crash. Books, journal, papers and knitting skidded in all directions. Estelle stood in the middle of them, red with anger. "It is *not* Nan Pilgrim!" she shouted. "Nan never harmed anyone in her life! It's you lot that do the harm, spreading tales all the time, you and Theresa and Karen. And I'm ashamed I was ever friends with Karen!"

Nan put her hot face in her hands. Estelle was a bit too loyal for comfort.

"Pick that desk up, Estelle," said Mr Wentworth.

Simon forgot himself and opened his mouth to make a jeering comment. Chrestomanci's eyes just happened to glance at him. Simon's mouth shut with a snap and his eyes popped.

And that was all the notice Chrestomanci took of the interruption. "If you will all attend," he said. Everyone did, immediately. "Thank you. Before we name the witch, I want you all to give the name of a second histori-cal personage. You in the front, you begin – er – um – Theresa – er – Fish."

Everyone had already given one name. Everyone was convinced that the Inquisitor would know the witch by the name they gave. It was obviously important not to name anybody wicked. So Theresa, although she was offended by the way the Inquisitor got her name wrong, thought very carefully indeed. And, as usually happens, her mind was instantly filled with all the villains in

History. She sat there dumbly, running through Burke and Hare, Crippen, Judas Iscariot, Nero and Torquemada, and quite unable to think of anybody good.

"Come along – er – Tatiana," said Chrestomanci.

"Theresa," said Theresa. And then, with inspiration, "*Saint* Theresa, I mean."

Chrestomanci wrote that down in his gold notebook and pointed to Delia. "Saint George," said Delia.

"Didn't exist in any world," said Chrestomanci. "Try again."

Delia racked her brains and eventually came up with Lady Godiva. Chrestomanci's pointing finger moved on round the class, causing everyone the same trouble. Villains poured through their minds – Attila the Hun, Richard III, Lucrezia Borgia, Joseph Stalin – and when they did manage to think of anyone less villainous, it always seemed to be people like Anne Boleyn or Galileo, who had been put to death. Most people did not like to mention those either, though Nirupam, because he knew Chrestomanci was not really an Inquisitor, took a risk and said Charles I. Chrestomanci turned to Mr Wentworth after most names were mentioned, and Mr Wentworth told him who they were. Most of 2Y could not think why the Inquisitor needed to do that, unless it was to prove that Mr Wentworth was a mastermind, but Nan thought, He's collecting symptoms again. Why? Somebody in History must be very important, I think.

Charles watched Chrestomanci's finger point towards him. He thought, You don't get me like that! "Saint Francis," he said. Chrestomanci's finger simply moved on to Dan Smith.

Dan was stumped. "Please, sir, I've got stomach ache. I can't think."

The finger went on pointing.

"Oh," said Dan. "Er – Dick Turpin."

This evoked a gasp from 2Y, and a near-groan of disappointment when Chrestomanci's finger moved on, across the gangway and pointed to Estelle.

Estelle had picked up her desk and most of her books by now, but her knitting wool had rolled under several desks and come unwound as it went. Estelle was on her knees reeling it in, greyer than ever, and did not notice. Nan leant down and poked her. Estelle jumped. "Is it me now? Sorry. Guy Fawkes – has anyone had Guy Fawkes yet?" She went back to her wool.

"One moment," said Chrestomanci. A curious hush seemed to grow in the room. "Can you tell me about Guy Fawkes?"

Estelle looked up again. Everyone was looking at her, wondering if she was the witch, but Estelle was only thinking about her wool. "Guy Fawkes?" she said. "They put him on a bone-fire for blowing up the Houses of Parliament."

"Blowing them *up*?" said Chrestomanci.

Simon opened his mouth to say Estelle was quite right, and shut it again hastily. Estelle nodded. A number of people called out, "Yes, sir. He did, sir!"

Chrestomanci looked at Mr Wentworth. Mr Wentworth said, "In 1605, Guy Fawkes was smuggled into the Parliament cellars with some kegs of gunpowder, in order to blow up the Government and the King. But he seems to have made a mistake. The gunpowder blew up in the night and destroyed both Houses, without killing anyone. Guy Fawkes got out unhurt, but they caught him almost at once."

It sounded like all the other times Mr Wentworth had told Chrestomanci a piece of History, but somehow it was not. Chrestomanci's eyes had a special gleam, very bright and black, and he looked straight at Nan as he remarked, "A mistake, eh? That doesn't surprise me. That fellow Fawkes never could get anything right." He pointed at Nan.

"Richard the Lionheart," said Nan. And she thought, He's got it! Guy Fawkes is the reason our world went dif-

193

ferent. But why? He'll want me to describe it and I don't know why. She thought and thought, while Chrestomanci was collecting names no one needed now from the rest of 2Y. 5 November 1605. All Nan could remember was something her mother had once said, long ago, before the Inquisitors took her away. Mum had said 5 November was the last day of Witch Week. Witch Week began on Hallowe'en, and today was Hallowe'en. Did that help? It must do, though Nan could not see how. But she knew she was right, and that Chrestomanci *had* found the answer, because he had such a smooth, pleased look as he stood beside Mr Wentworth.

"Now," he said. "We shall reveal the witch."

He had gone vague again. He was slowly fetching a slim golden case from a dove-grey pocket and, if he was looking at anyone, it was at Charles now. Good, thought Nan. He's giving me time to think. And Charles thought, All right. Reveal me then. But I'm still not going to help.

Chrestomanci held the flat gold box out so that everyone could see it. "This," he said, "is the very latest modern witch-finder. Look at it carefully." Charles did. He was almost certain that the witch-finder was a gold cigarette case. "When I let go of this machine," Chrestomanci said, "it will travel by itself through the air, and it will point to everyone in turn, except Simon. When it points to a witch, it is programmed to make a noise. I want the witch it points to to come and stand beside me."

2Y stared at the gold oblong, tense and excited. There were gasps. It had bobbed in Chrestomanci's hand. Chrestomanci let go of it and it stayed in the air, bobbing about by itself. Charles glowered. He understood. Brian. Brian was going to carry it invisibly round. That did it! If Chrestomanci thought he could get round Charles by giving Brian all the fun, he was going to be really disappointed.

194

The bobbing case upended itself. Charles saw it split open a fraction along the top edge, as Brian took a quick peep to see if it was indeed a cigarette case. It was. Charles glimpsed white cigarettes in it.

"Off you go," Chrestomanci said to it.

The gold box shut with a loud snap, making everybody jump, and then travelled swiftly to the first desk. It stopped level with Ronald West's head. It gave out a shrill beeping-sound. Everybody jumped again, including Ronald and the gold box.

"Come out here," Chrestomanci said.

Ronald, looking quite dumbfounded, got out of his desk and stumbled towards Chrestomanci. "I never —!" he protested.

"Yes you are, you know," Chrestomanci said. And he said to the gold box, "Carry on."

A little uncertainly, the box travelled to Geoffrey Baines. It beeped again. Chrestomanci beckoned. Out came Geoffrey, white-faced but not protesting.

"How did it know?" he said drearily.

"Modern technology," said Chrestomanci.

This time the gold box went on without being told. It beeped, moved, and beeped again. Person after person got miserably up and trailed out to the front. Charles thought it was a dirty trick. Chrestomanci was just trying to break his nerve. The box was level with Lance Osgood now. Everyone waited for it to beep. And waited. The box stayed beside Lance, pointing until Lance's eyes were crossed with looking at it. But nothing happened.

"Go on," said Chrestomanci. "He's not a witch."

The box moved to Dan Smith. Here, it made the longest, loudest noise yet. Dan blenched. "I covered up my tracks!" he said.

"Out here," said Chrestomanci.

Dan got up slowly. "It's not fair! My stomach aches."

"No doubt you deserve it," said Chrestomanci. "By

195

the noise, you've used witchcraft quite recently. What did you do?"

"Only hid a pair of running-shoes," Dan mumbled. He did not look at Charles as he slouched up the gangway. Charles did not look at Dan either. He was beginning to see that Chrestomanci was not pretending that people were witches.

By now, the front of the class was quite crowded. The box went to Nirupam next. Nirupam was waiting for it. It beeped even louder for him than it had for Dan. The moment it did, Nirupam got up and fled with long strides to the front of the room, in order not to be asked what witchcraft he had done. Then the box came to Charles. The noise was deafening.

"All right, all right!" Charles muttered. He too trudged to the front of the class. So Chrestomanci was playing fair, but he was still obviously trying to teach Charles a lesson by devaluing witchcraft. Charles looked round the other people standing out in front. He knew his was the strongest magic of the lot. And he wanted to keep it. There were still a thousand things he could do with it. He did not want to blend with another world, even if they did not burn witches there. As to being burnt – Charles looked down at his blister – he found he rather enjoyed being frightened, once he got used to it. It made life interesting.

Meanwhile, the gold box followed Charles down the gangway and pointed to Delia. There was silence. Delia did not try to hide her smirk. But the smirk came off her face when the box moved to Theresa. It gave one small clear beep.

Theresa stood up, scandalized. "Who? *Me!*"

"Only a very small, third-grade sort of witch," Chrestomanci told her comfortingly.

It did not comfort Theresa in the least. If she was to be a witch, she felt she should at least be a first-class one. It was a disgrace either way. She was really angry when the

196

box moved to Karen and did not beep for Karen either. But she was equally annoyed when the box went on and beeped for Heather, Deborah and all her other friends. She stood there with the most dreadful mixed feelings.

Then the box beeped for Estelle too. Theresa tossed her head angrily. But Estelle sprang up beaming. "Oh good! I'm a witch! I'm a witch!" She skipped out to the front, grinning all over her face.

"Some people!" Theresa said unconvincingly.

Estelle did not care. She laughed when the box beeped loudly for Nan and Nan came thoughtfully to join her. "I think most people in the world must be witches," Estelle whispered to her. Nan nodded. She was sure it was true. She was sure this fitted in with all the other things Chrestomanci had discovered, but she still could not think how to explain it.

This left four people scattered about the room. They were all, even Simon, looking peevish and left-out.

"It's not fair!" said Karen.

"At least *we* won't be burnt," said Delia.

Chrestomanci beckoned to the box. It wandered up the gangway and put itself in his hand. Chrestomanci put it back in his pocket while he looked round the crowd of witches. He ignored Charles. He had given him up. He looked at Nan and then across at Mr Wentworth, who had been crowded against the door in the crush. "Well, Wentworth," he said. "This looks quite promising, doesn't it? We've got a fair amount of witchcraft to draw on here. I suggest we make our push now. If Nan is ready to explain to everyone —"

Nan was nothing like ready. She was about to say so, when the classroom door flew open. Mr Wentworth was barged aside. And Miss Cadwallader stood in his place, stiff and upright and stringy with anger.

"What are you all doing, 2Y?" she said. "Back to your seats with the utmost rapidity."

Mr Wentworth was behind the door, white and

shaking. Everyone looked doubtfully at Chrestomanci. He had gone very vague. So everybody did the prudent thing and scuttled back to their desks. As they went, three more people came into the room behind Miss Cadwallader.

Miss Cadwallader faced Chrestomanci in angry triumph. "Mr Chant," she said, "you are an imposter. Here is the real Inquisitor. Inquisitor Littleton." She stood aside and shut the door, so that everyone could see the Inquisitor.

Inquisitor Littleton was a small man in a blue pinstriped suit. He had a huge man on either side of him in the black uniform of the Inquisition. Each of these huge men had a gun holster, a truncheon and a folded whip in his belt. At the sight of them, Charles's burnt finger doubled itself up and hid inside his fist like a guilty secret.

"You move, and I'll order you shot!" Inquisitor Littleton snapped at Chrestomanci. His voice was harsh. His little watery eyes glared at Chrestomanci from a little blunt face covered with bright red veins. His blue suit did not fit him very well, as if Inquisitor Littleton had shrunk and hardened some time after the suit was bought, into a new shape, dense with power.

"Good afternoon, Inquisitor," Chrestomanci said politely. "I'd been half expecting you." He looked across his shoulder, to Simon. "Nod, if I'm right," he said. "Did you say an Inquisitor would be here before lunch?"

Simon nodded, looking shattered.

Inquisitor Littleton narrowed his watery eyes. "So it was witchcraft that made my car break down?" he said. "I knew it!" He unslung a black box he was carrying on a strap over his shoulder. He pointed it at Chrestomanci and turned a knob. Everyone saw the violent twitching of the dials on top. "Thought so," grated Inquisitor Littleton. "It's a witch." He jerked his blunt chin at Mr Wentworth. "Now get me that one."

One of the huge men reached out a huge hand and dragged Mr Wentworth over from beside the door as easily as if Mr Wentworth had been a guy stuffed with straw. Miss Cadwallader looked as if she would like to protest about this, but she gave it up as useless. Inquisitor Littleton trained his black box on Mr Wentworth.

Before he could turn the knob, the black box was torn out of his hands. With its broken strap trailing, it hurried from the Inquisitor to Chrestomanci.

"I think that was a mistake, Brian," said Chrestomanci.

Both huge men drew their guns. Inquisitor Littleton backed away and pointed at Chrestomanci. His face was purple, and full of a queer mixture of hate and horror and pleasure. "Look at that!" he shouted out. "It has a demon to wait on it! Oh, I've got you now!"

Chrestomanci looked almost irritated. "My good man," he said, "that really is a most ignorant assumption. Only a hedge wizard would stoop to using a demon."

"I'm not a demon!" shouted Brian's shrill voice. "I'm Brian Wentworth!"

Delia screamed. The huge man who was not holding Mr Wentworth seemed to lose his nerve. Glaring with fear, he held his gun out in both hands, and aimed it at the black box.

"Throw it!" said Chrestomanci.

Brian obeyed. The black box sailed towards the window. The huge man was muddled into following it round with his gun. He fired. There was a tremendous crash. Quite a few people screamed this time. The black box exploded into a muddle of wire and metal plates and half of the window blew out. A gust of rain blew in.

"You fool!" said Inquisitor Littleton. "That was my very latest model witch-finder!" He glared at Chrestomanci. "Right. I've had enough of this foul thing. Get it for me."

The huge man put his gun back in its holster and marched towards Chrestomanci. Nirupam quickly stuck up a long arm. "Please. Just a moment. I think Miss Cadwallader may be a witch too."

Everyone at once looked at Miss Cadwallader. She said, "How dare you, child!" but she was as white as Mr Wentworth.

And this, Nan realized, was where she came in. She was not sure how, but she surged to her feet all the same, in such haste that she nearly knocked her desk over like Estelle. Everyone stared at her. Nan felt terrible. For a long, long instant, she went on standing there without a thought in her head and without one scrap of confidence to help her. But she knew she could not just sit down again. She began to talk.

"Just a moment," she said. "Before you do another thing, I've got to tell you about Guy Fawkes. He's the reason almost everybody in the world is a witch, you know. The main thing about Guy Fawkes is that he was the kind of man who can never do anything right. He meant well, but he was a failure —"

"Make that girl shut up!" Inquisitor Littleton said, in his harsh bossy voice. Nan looked at him nervously, and then at the two huge men. None of them moved. In fact, now she looked, everyone seemed to be stuck and frozen exactly where they were when she first stood up. She looked at Chrestomanci. He was staring vaguely into distance and did not seem to be doing anything either, but Nan was suddenly sure that Chrestomanci was somehow holding everything in one place to give her a chance to explain. That made her feel much better.

She had gone on talking all the time she was looking round, explaining about the Gunpowder Plot, and what a mistake the conspirators made choosing Guy Fawkes to do the blowing up. Now she seemed to be going on to explain about other worlds.

"There were an awful lot of Guy Fawkeses in an awful

200

lot of worlds," she heard herself saying. "And he was a failure in every one. Some people are like that. There are millions of other worlds, you know. The big differences get made at the big events in History, where a battle gets either won or lost. Both things can't happen in one world, so a new one splits off and goes different after that. But there are all sorts of smaller things that can go two ways as well, which *don't* make a world split off. You've probably all had those kind of dreams that are like your usual life, except that a lot of things are not the same, and you seem to know the future in them. Well, this is because these other worlds where two things can happen spread out from our own world like rainbows, and sort of flow into one another —"

Nan found herself rather admiring this description. She was inspired now. She could have talked for hours. But there was not much point unless she could persuade the rest of 2Y to *do* something. Everyone was just staring at her.

"Now our world should really just be a rainbow stripe in another proper world," she said. "But it isn't. And I'm going to tell you why, so that we can all do something about it. I told you Guy Fawkes was a failure. Well, the trouble was, he knew he was. And that made him very nervous, because he wanted to do at least this one thing right and blow up Parliament properly. He kept going over in his mind all the things that could go wrong: he could be betrayed, or the gunpowder would be damp, or his candle would go out, or his fuse wouldn't light – he thought of all the possibilities, all the things that make the rainbow-stripes of not-quite-different worlds. And in the middle of the night, he got so nervous that he went and lit the fuse, just to make sure it would light. He wasn't thinking that 5 November, the day he was doing it, was the last day of Witch Week, when there is so much magic around in the world that all sorts of peculiar things happen —"

201

"Will somebody silence that girl!" said Inquisitor Littleton.

He made Charles jump. Charles had been sitting all this time trying to understand the way he was feeling. He seemed to have divided into two again, but inside himself, where it did not show. Half of him was plain terrified. It felt as if it had been buried alive, in screaming, shut-in despair. The other half was angry, angry with Chrestomanci, Miss Cadwallader, 2Y, Inquisitor Littleton – everything. Now, when Inquisitor Littleton suddenly spoke in his loud grating voice, Charles looked at the Inquisitor. He was a small man with a stupid face, in a blue suit which did not fit, who enjoyed arresting witches.

Charles found himself remembering his first witch again. The fat man who had been so astonished at being burnt. And he suddenly understood the witch's amazement. It was because someone so ordinary, so plain stupid, as Inquisitor Littleton had the power to burn him. And that was all wrong.

"Oh come on, all of you!" said Nan. "Don't you see? When Guy Fawkes lit that fuse, that made a new spread of rainbow possibilities. In our proper world, the world we ought to belong to, the fuse should have gone straight out again, and the Houses of Parliament would have been perfectly safe. But once the fuse was alight, the night watchman could have smelt it, or Guy Fawkes could have put it out with water, or the thing could have happened which made us the way we are. Guy Fawkes could have stamped the fuse out, but left just one tiny spark alight, which went on burning and creeping towards the kegs of gunpowder —"

"I told you to shut that girl up!" said Inquisitor Littleton.

Charles was in one piece again now. He looked from the Inquisitor to Chrestomanci. Chrestomanci did not look so elegant just then. His suit was crumpled as if he

202

had fallen away inside it, and his face was pale and hollow. Charles could see sweat on his forehead. And he understood that Chrestomanci was putting out a huge effort and somehow holding the whole world still, to give Nan time to persuade 2Y to use their combined witchcraft to change it. But 2Y were still sitting there like dumb things. That was why Inquisitor Littleton had started talking again. He was obviously one of those people who were very hard to keep quiet, and Chrestomanci had had to let go of him in order to have strength to hold everything else.

"Will you be quiet, girl!" said Inquisitor Littleton.

"BOOM!" said Nan. "And up went Parliament, but with no people in it. It wasn't very important, because even Guy Fawkes wasn't killed. But remember it was Witch Week. That made it a much worse explosion than it should have been. In it, this whole stripe of the rainbow, where we are now, and all the magic anywhere near, got blown out of the rest of the world, like a sort of long coloured splinter. But it wasn't blown quite free. It was still joined to the rest of the rainbow at both ends. And that's the way it still is. And we could put it back if only we could make it so that the explosion never happened. And because it's Hallowe'en today, and there's even more magic about than usual —"

Charles saw that Chrestomanci was beginning to shake. He looked tired out. At this rate, Chrestomanci was not going to have any strength left to put their splinter of world back where it belonged. Charles jumped up. He wanted to apologize. It was obvious that someone with power like Chrestomanci's could easily have just gone away the moment Inquisitor Littleton arrived. Instead, he had chosen to stay and help them. But saying sorry would have to wait. Charles knew he had to do something. And thanks to Nan, he knew just what to do.

"Sit down, boy!" rasped Inquisitor Littleton.

Charles took no notice. He dived across the gangway and took hold of Simon Silverson by the front of his blazer. "Simon. Say what Guy Fawkes did. Quick!"

Simon gazed at Charles. He shook his head and pointed to his mouth.

"Go on! Say it, you fool!" said Charles, and he shook Simon.

Simon kept his mouth shut. He was afraid to say anything. It was like a bad dream. "Say what Guy Fawkes did!" Charles yelled at him. He gave up shaking Simon and poured witchcraft at him to make him say it. And Simon just shook his head.

Nirupam saw the point. "Say it, Simon!" he said. And that made all the rest of 2Y understand what Charles was trying to do. Everyone stood up in their seats and shouted at Simon: "SAY IT, SIMON!" Mr Wentworth shouted. Brian's voice joined in. Witchcraft was blasting at Simon from all sides, and even Karen and Delia were shouting at him. Nan joined in the shouting. She was bubbling with pride and delight. She had done this, just by describing what happened. It was as good as witchcraft any day. "SAY IT, SIMON!" everyone screamed.

Simon opened his mouth. "I – Oh, leave *off*!" He was terrified of what might happen, but once he had started to speak, all the witchcraft beating at him was too much for him. "He – he – Guy Fawkes blew up the Houses of Parliament."

Everything at once began to ripple.

It was as if the world had turned into a vast curtain, hanging in folds, with every fold in it rippling in and out. The ripples ran through desks, windows, walls and people alike. Each person was rippled through. They were tugged, and rippled again, until everyone felt they were coming to pieces. By then, the ripples were so strong and steep that everyone could see right down into the folds. For just a moment, on the outside of each fold, was the classroom everyone knew, with the Inquisitor and his huge men on the same fold as Miss Cadwallader, and Chrestomanci on another fold beside them. The inner parts of the folds were all different places.

Charles realized that if he was going to apologize to Chrestomanci, he had better do it at once. He turned round to say it. But the folds had already rippled flat and nothing was the same any more.

Chapter Sixteen

"I'm very sorry, sir," said one of the boys. He sounded as if he meant it, for a wonder.

Mr Crossley jumped, and wondered if he had been asleep. He seemed to have had that kind of shiver that makes you say "Someone walked over my grave." He looked up from the books he was marking.

The janitor was in the classroom. What was his name? He had a raucous voice and a lot of stupid opinions. Littleton, that was it. Littleton seemed to be clearing up broken glass. Mr Crossley was puzzled, because he did not remember a window being broken. But when he looked over at the windows, he saw one of them was newly mended, with a lot of putty and many thumbprints.

"There you are, Mr Crossley. All tidy now," Mr Littleton rasped.

"Thank you, Littleton," Mr Crossley said coldly. If you let Littleton get talking, he stayed and tried to teach the class. He watched the janitor collect his things and back himself through the door. Thank goodness!

"Thank you, Charles," said someone.

Mr Crossley jerked round and discovered a total stranger in the room. This man was tall and tired-looking and seemed, from his clothes, to be on his way to a wedding. Mr Crossley thought he must be a school governor and started to stand up politely.

"Oh, please don't get up," Chrestomanci said. "I'm just on my way out." He walked to the door. Before he went out of it, he looked round 2Y and said, "If any of you want me again, a message to the Old Gate House should find me."

The door closed behind him. Mr Crossley sat down to his marking again. He stared. There was a note on top of the topmost exercise book. He knew it had not been there before. It was written in ordinary blue ballpoint, in capital letters, and it gave Mr Crossley the oddest feeling of having been in the same situation before. Why was that? He must have dozed off and had a dream. Yes. Now Mr Crossley thought about it, he *had* had the strangest dream. He had dreamed he taught in a dreadful boarding school called Larwood House. He looked thankfully up at the bent, busy heads of 2Y. This was, as he well knew, Portway Oaks Comprehensive, and everyone went home every evening. Thank goodness! Mr Crossley hated the idea of teaching in a boarding school. You were always on the job.

He wondered who had written the note. And here, as his eyes went over the class, he had a momentary feeling of shock. A lot of faces were missing from his dream. He remembered a batch of tiresome girls: Theresa Mullett, Delia Martin, Heather Something, Karen Something Else. None of them were there. Nor was Daniel Smith.

Ah but—Mr Crossley remembered now. Dan Smith should have been there. He was in hospital. Two days ago, the stupid boy had eaten a handful of tintacks for a bet. No one had believed he had, at first. But when Mr Wentworth, the Headmaster, had put Dan in his car and driven him to be X-rayed, there he was, full of tintacks. Idiots some boys were!

And here was another mad thing about Mr Crossley's dream: he had dreamt that Miss Cadwallader was Head in place of Mr Wentworth! Quite mad. Mr Crossley knew perfectly well that Miss Cadwallader was the lady who ran The Gate House School for Girls, where Eileen Hodge was a teacher. Come to think of it, that must have

207

been why he dreamt of Theresa Mullett and her friends. He had seen their faces staring out at him from the prim line of girls walking behind Eileen Hodge.

And now Mr Crossley remembered something else that almost made him forget his dream and the mysterious note. Eileen Hodge had at last agreed to go out with him. He was to call for her on Tuesday, because she was going away for half-term. He was getting somewhere there at last!

But even through his pleasure about Eileen, the dream and the note kept nagging at Mr Crossley. Why should it bother him who had written the note? He looked at Brian Wentworth, sitting next to his great friend Simon Silverson. The two of them were giggling about something. The note was quite probably one of Brian's jokes. But it could equally well be some deep scheme masterminded by Charles Morgan and Nirupam Singh. Mr Crossley looked at those two.

Charles looked back at Mr Crossley over his glasses and across the piece of paper he was supposed to be writing on. How much did Mr Crossley know? Charles's writing had got no further than the title: *Hallowe'en Poem*. Neither had Nirupam's. On the floor between them was a pair of spiked running-shoes and, filling them with wonder, was the name marked on the shoes: *Daniel Smith*. Both of them knew that Dan did not own any running-shoes. Of course, Smith was not exactly an uncommon name, but – both of them were struggling with strange double memories.

Charles wondered particularly at the sense of relief and peace he had. He felt at ease inside. He also felt rather hungry. One part of his memory told him that this was because Brian Wentworth had invisibly eaten half his lunch. The other half suggested that it was because chess club had taken up most of the dinner hour. And here was an odd thing. Up till that moment, Charles had intended to be a chess grand master. Now those double memories caused him to change his mind. Someone – whose name he could not quite remember now – had suggested to him that he was going to have a very strong talent indeed for something, and it was not for chess, Charles was sure now. Perhaps he would be an inventor instead. Anyway, the chess club half of his memory, which seemed to be the important half, suggested that he hurried home early so he could eat the last of the corn-flakes before his sister Bernadine hogged them.

"Guy Fawkes," Nirupam murmured.

Charles did not know if Nirupam was referring to witchcraft, or to Dan Smith's idea for half-term. They had been going to collect money for the guy, using Nirupam for a guy. Nirupam, in the Morgans' old push-chair, made a beautiful long, thin, floppy guy. Now they were both wondering if they would have the nerve to do it on their own, without Dan to keep them up to it.

"Why did you have to bet Dan he couldn't eat tintacks?" Charles whispered to Nirupam.

"Because I didn't think he would!" Nirupam answered grumpily. He had been in a lot of trouble with Mr Wentworth about that bet. "Could we get Estelle and Nan to help push me?"

"They're girls," Charles objected. But he considered the idea while he underlined *Hallowe'en Poem* in red ink, with blood-drops. Those two girls might just do it, at that. As he inked the last drop of blood, he noticed a blister on his finger. It had reached the flat, white, empty stage by now. Carefully, Charles inked it bright red. He was not sure he wanted to forget about things that soon.

Mr Crossley was still considering the note. It could be another flight of fancy from Nan Pilgrim. Nan, as usual, since she had arrived at the school from Essex at the beginning of term, was sitting next to Estelle Green. They were thick as thieves, those two. A good thing, because Estelle had been rather lonely before Nan arrived.

Nan glanced up at Mr Crossley, and down again at her pen rushing across her paper. Fascinated, she read: *And in this part of the rainbow, Guy Fawkes stamped the fuse out, but a little, tiny smouldering spark remained. The spark crept and ate its way to the kegs of gunpowder. BOOM!!!*

"Estelle! Look at this!"

Estelle leaned over, looked, and goggled. "Do you know what I think?" she whispered. "When you grow up to be an author and write books, you'll think you're making the books up, but they'll all really be true, somewhere." She sighed. "My poem's going to be about a great enchanter."

Mr Crossley suddenly wondered why he was worrying about the note. It was only a joke, after all. He cleared his throat. Everyone looked up hopefully. "Somebody," said Mr Crossley, "seems to have sent me a Hallowe'en message." And he read out the note. *"SOMEONE IN THIS CLASS IS A WITCH."*

2Y thought this was splendid news. Hands shot up all over the room like a bed of beansprouts.

"It's me, Mr Crossley!"

"Mr Crossley, I'm the witch!"

"Can I be the witch, Mr Crossley?"

"Me, Mr Crossley, me, me, me!"